SPRING WARRIOR

THE WYTH COURTS BOOK 2

JULIANA HAYGERT

COPYRIGHT

Manufactured in the United States of America.

First Edition December 2019

www.jsdark.com

Edited by Hot Tree Editing

Proofreading by Rare Bird Editing

Cover design by The Book Brander

❀ Created with Vellum

SPRING WARRIOR

He thought all was lost ... until he found her.

Civil war sliced through the Spring Court, leaving the royal family assassinated and General Ashton imprisoned. Torturous years later, Ash finally escapes and embarks on a mission to complete the last order he was given by the late King—to locate his lost princess.

In a small flower shop, living a rather mundane existence, he finds a rare beauty named Hayley—who happens to be the rightful heir to the throne. It falls to Ash to convince her to accompany him back to the Spring Court and challenge the faux king for the crown.

Hayley's only chance at survival is to stay close to the chiseled warrior's side, even as they reignite the flames of war. Can Ash help her tap into the strength of her royal blood and awaken the queen within before the faux king tears them, and what's left of their kingdom, apart?

Spring Warrior is a standalone steamy paranormal romance with a HEA. Each book in the Wyth Courts series will feature a different couple, with a complete story, and a HEA. Suited for readers 18+ due to language and sex scenes.

AUTHOR'S NOTE

I HOPE you enjoy reading *Spring Warrior*!

IF YOU WANT to know about new releases, upcoming books, giveaways, and more, don't forget to sign up for my Newsletter!

Want to see exclusive teasers, help me decide on covers, read excerpts, talk about books, etc? Then join my reader group on Facebook: Juliana's Club!

1

ASHTON

THE WHIP CRACKED and struck my back.

I gritted my teeth, but endured the pain, as I had been doing for almost fifteen years. I would have believed that, after being whipped thousands of times, I wouldn't feel it anymore, but every time a new session started, the pain came back as if it were for the blooming first time.

But I preferred when they whipped me to the other kinds of torture I had to endure when they were in a bad mood—which was often.

"How many was that?" Rabi asked, a nasty tone to his voice. He was the dungeon master here and the one who got to torture me. He loved seeing me squirm under his whip, which was why I tried my best to stay quiet, but sometimes... sometimes the whip crashed just right, worsening an already open wound. "Twenty? Forty? Maybe a hundred?" he teased.

I didn't know, because I never counted them. If I counted them, they hurt more. So I just gritted my teeth and tried keeping my mind blank. I found that was the least painful way.

The whip paused. "General Ashton, do you pledge your alliance to the Spring King?"

They asked me that at least five times a day. By now, they should know my answer by heart, but they insisted on it.

"Never," I answered through my clenched teeth. "Just kill me."

Rabi snorted. "I would love to, but the king wants you alive."

Why? Why the blossom did that bastard still want me alive? Hadn't they learned by now that I would never change? That I would never say a word? I didn't know why they wasted their time with me.

The whip cracked one more time, and I felt the blood sliding down my legs and soaking my ragged pants. "There." Rabi wound the whip around his arm and stood in front of me. "That should soften you up."

Holy petals, I knew what that meant.

The fake king was coming, and he would conduct the next round of torture while asking me questions.

Bile rose to my throat. I wasn't afraid of Vasant and the torture, no. What I loathed was staying in the same room as the male fae who called himself the Spring King—as if killing his older brother and his entire family and stealing the crown was enough to be worthy of the title.

Rabi nodded to the guards standing at the corners of the room. They unhooked the chains from the anchor on the walls and tugged on the metal clasps around my wrists, pulling me with them. Hurt and a little dizzy because of the blood loss, I tripped on my own feet, causing them to laugh, of course.

When I was first captured fifteen years ago, I fought back every second of the day, week, month.... I didn't know when exactly I had stopped fighting, but for a long time, I resisted. When they pulled me, I pulled back; when they struck me, I jerked against the chains and tried to strike back. When they laughed, I jumped on them, at least as far as my chains let me go.

Then months turned into years and all hope of ever escaping was lost.

I only knew that soon would be my fifteenth anniversary in here because I marked down the days on the stone walls of my cell.

The guards led me down a dark corridor until it opened in a large, round area full of thick metal doors. Down here, nothing was made of wood or earth—that would have made it too easy to escape.

No, they had thick, metal-infused stones and lots of iron, which hurt us to touch and could poison us with prolonged use.

They loved torturing me with iron.

As they threw me in my small cell and locked the doors, I wondered what Vasant would do with me today. Torture by iron? Fire? Water? Or simply by beating me up until my bones broke?

I scooted to the back of the cell, where a dirty rag that served as my bed was spread over the hard, stone floor, and rested my back on the wall. I glanced up, imagining a window there and the sunlight streaming through it, bathing my skin with warmth.

I hadn't seen the sun since I had been brought down here.

I hadn't seen anything but these cold, dark walls and hallways in almost fifteen years.

I closed my eyes, and the images came back like a flood.

The moment the traitor let Vasant and his forces inside

the castle, taking us by surprise. I was struck and held back while Vasant advanced and killed King Eden. Queen Elowen screamed when they turned to her and her children, Wells and Ayla.

It all happened so fast, but I still remembered... the pain, the agony, the despair that lasted for a million years. The royal family was assassinated and most of my soldiers massacred around me, and all I could do was watch.

I brought my bound hands to my chest and rubbed at my still hurting heart.

This pain on the inside wouldn't ever go way, not until I died.

For leaves' sake, how I wished I could die.

I glanced around the cell. There was nothing here I could use to kill myself. The time I had tried taking off my pants and using them to hang myself, they were so raggedy, they ripped with my weight. Another time, I tried attacking Rabi so I could snatch his knife from his hands, but I was subdued before I could pierce my chest.

As a warrior, I had failed miserably. My honor had vanished. I had no reason to live anymore.

I closed my eyes again and wished that my sword were here with me.

The sound of metal clanking on the ground startled me. My eyes shot open, and I gasped.

My sword.

It was at my feet.

And behind the sword was Mahaeru, one of the goddesses of Wyth.

I stared at her, sure I was hallucinating.

"Didn't you wish for your sword?" Mahaeru asked, her voice tight. She was one of three sisters, the harshest and most severe of them. Her black hair was tied in a bun at the nape of her neck, and she wore black clothes that reminded me of a soldier's uniform. "Here it is."

I blinked. "How...? Why...?"

She waved her hand, and the metal clasps around my wrists fell to the ground. "We don't have time for chitchat. Get up."

I inhaled deeply as I felt it—my power slowly awaking from a long slumber. Now that the clasps were gone, I could use my magic again.

With my hand on the wall for balance, I pushed to my feet. "Why are you here?"

"It's time, General Ashton," she said. "Eden's daughter has come of age."

I gaped at her, confused. Then, as if she had opened a gate inside my mind, I remembered it. A couple of months before his death, King Eden told me a secret: he had a daughter with a human female. He had sent them back to Earth, afraid of his wife's wrath if she found out about them. He had wanted me to know because, if something happened to him and his children during this long and bloody war, his daughter was the only one who could claim the throne of the Spring Court.

I had forgotten about all of this, because how could I help her when I was locked in here?

"You want me to find her," I whispered, still in shock.

"Not just find her," Mahaeru said. "You have to bring her back. If you don't, terrible things will happen, not only to the Spring Court, but to the entire Wyth." She handed me a clean shirt and shoes. "Put them on. You'll need at least shoes to run." She waved her hand again, and I felt her magic brushing against my skin. "I'm putting a strong soldier glamour over you. Don't stall for too long and don't let anyone touch you, and you won't be found out." She waved her hand to the side, and the cell's door opened. "Now go."

I stared at the goddess. She wanted me to go, but where? Wasn't King Eden's daughter on Earth? How would I get there?

Footsteps echoed from the hallway.

"Go! Quickly!" She shooed me away.

Enough hesitation.

I shoved my feet in the boots, picked up my sword, and ran out of the cell.

"HERE YOU GO, MRS. SMITH," I said, handing out the bouquet of pink, orange, and red roses to the old woman.

Mrs. Smith took the bouquet and smiled at me. "Gorgeous as always, my dear. Thank you." She started for the door.

"Tell Grace congratulations for me!" I waved at her.

She glanced over her shoulder at me. "I will. Thank you again."

The old woman exited the shop, and I continued smiling, amazed at how time flew by. I remembered when her granddaughter Grace was a shy girl first starting high school. I was a senior back then, but since Mrs. Smith was a regular client of my mother's flower shop and I knew about her, I approached her and introduced her to some girls from her grade who lived in my neighborhood.

Now, four years later, she was a gorgeous ballerina in a big dance competition. Odds were she would win it, and Mrs. Smith would be there to see it and congratulate her with the rose bouquet.

Though I had a green thumb, I didn't have any special talents like that. Sometimes I envied people like Grace. But then I glanced around the shop and smiled again.

It was fine if I didn't have any special talents, because the shop was going so well.

Before I was born, my mother was a singer. She taught music for a couple of years, but when we moved to Greendale when I was five, she opened the flower shop.

Though the first year was hard because we were a new store in a small town, people soon fell in love with our flowers and plants, which for some reason always lasted longer than normal—my mother always said it was because of my green thumb—and business grew.

And because flowers and plants brought me joy, I didn't want to do anything else with my life.

The bell over the door chimed.

"Welcome to—" I glanced to the door and the words died on my tongue. "What the hell are you doing here?"

Peter strolled to the counter and smiled at me. "Hi, Hayley, how is it going?"

I frowned, taking a step back. Even though there was a tall, wooden counter between us, I didn't want to be anywhere near him. "It was great, until you came in."

"Aw, don't say that, babe."

"Don't 'babe' me," I said through gritted teeth. "I'm not your babe anymore." Not since he decided to cheat on me with some bimbo a few months ago. He had probably always cheated on me, but I only found out recently, when I went to his college to spend the weekend with him. I wanted to surprise him since it had been a few weeks since we had last seen each other. But when I arrived there, he was half naked with a girl in his dorm. "If you're not here to buy some flowers, please leave."

He leaned over the counter, giving me his sly smile, the same one I thought was charming for over three years. "Hear me out, babe—"

"Don't 'babe' me."

"—I'm going to the beach for spring break tomorrow, and I decided to stop in town and see if you want to go with me," he said, his voice so cool, so gentle. If I didn't know better, I would have fallen for it. "I thought that, with this trip, we can rekindle things, you know?" He reached over the counter for me. "I've missed you, babe."

"I said don't 'babe' me!" I slapped his hand away. "Seriously, Peter, I don't know what you're going for here. You really think I would accept this invitation? Do you think I'm that naive?"

"But, babe—"

"Holy shit, Peter, stop with this freaking 'babe' thing!" I grabbed my phone from the shelf behind me. "I want you to leave right now. If you don't, I'll call the police."

He snorted. "You're joking."

I unlocked my phone and opened the phone app. "Am I?"

"What are you going to tell them? That your boyfriend is asking you to go on a trip with him and you don't want to?"

"No, I'll say you're harassing me."

"Babe, that's going too far. Why don't we—"

"Leave, Peter." My mother appeared from the back room and faced my ex as if she were a freaking general. She had been out on deliveries, but thank goodness she arrived right on time. "Or *I* will call the police."

Peter hesitated but took a step back. He had always been

afraid of my mother, even though she was at least a head shorter than him. "Just... I'm leaving tomorrow morning, Hayley. If you change your mind, you know where to find me."

He ducked out of the store, and I turned to my mother. "Thank you."

"Anytime," she said with a forced shiver. "Anything to keep that creep away."

I smiled. She had never been a fan of Peter. I knew she had wanted to say "I told you so" when I found out he was cheating on me.

"I confess, I'm really surprised to see him here," I said, looking at the door again. I had given him such a hard time after our breakup, that when he finally stopped coming after me and apologizing, I had thought it was for good. "I don't know why he's wasting his time. He should have gone to the beach already."

My mother picked up a notepad from the shelf. "Speaking of bitch, where's Sarah?"

"Mom!" I laughed.

She shrugged. "What? She always says she's a cool bitch."

I shook my head. Sarah had been my best friend since our first year of elementary school, and she loved my mother probably more than she loved her family. To be honest, when she left town to attend a big college, I thought she was sadder about leaving my mother behind than me.

"That bitch went to the beach too."

My mother put down the notepad and stared at me. "You should go too."

I almost choked on air. "What? With Peter?"

"No, not with that jerk, but with Sarah," she said. "I mean, you're young, you're in college too. That's what kids your age do at this time of the year. You should go."

I stared at her, a little confused. I was taking a low residency business degree online because I didn't want to move out of Greendale, where our family business was located, and leave her alone to take care of it. I wouldn't leave it all behind now.

"No, I can't," I said. "It's spring. The shop is booming. I can't leave you alone during the busiest time of the year."

"Nonsense. I can handle the store by myself for one week." She stretched her arms wide. "I promise you that everything will be intact when you get back."

I opened my mouth, but no words came out.

Right now, I felt a hundred years old. Where was the Hayley who spent late nights with her friends? Who went to parties with Sarah or Peter? Who wasn't the most popular girl in school but had been invited to all parties and went to most of them?

For a moment, I missed that Hayley.

But things changed. I started college and saw an opportunity with our store, and I embraced it. If things continued to grow, we would soon need a bigger place or a second store.

I was happy this way.

But seeing as my mother watched me with her hawk eyes, I just said, "I'll think about it."

3

I KNEW Evergreen Castle better than the palm of my hand. Holy petal, I knew the entire Spring Court inch by inch. Disguised as one of their soldiers, it was easy to slip out of the dungeons and out in the castle's courtyards.

After my first step outside, I stopped, my eyes shut tight. Too much light. The sun was shining bright, and it hurt my eyes. Slowly, I took a deep breath—the first lungful of fresh air in almost fifteen years—and opened my eyes.

I looked up at the blue skies, amazed I was finally out. After a few months of being treated worse than a rabid rat, I had assumed I would die down there in the dungeons—filthy, starving, cold, and alone.

As I followed the wooden path that wrapped around the castle, I glanced all around, a little relieved Vasant hadn't destroyed the green lawns, the colorful flowers, the vines that wrapped around the castle's walls. For some reason, I thought he would have brought chaos and darkness everywhere.

That didn't matter. He was still evil and heartless. Not worthy of the throne.

I trudged on toward the inner gate but halted a few yards from it, staring at the magically reinforced wooden walls and the large wooden gate, which, at this time of the day, was half-open. But what gave me pause was not the gate itself or the many soldiers in their dark green uniforms and long spears.

I paused because Xuan stood beside the gate, talking to some soldiers.

Xuan, who once had been a decorated general under King Eden, but had betrayed him and embraced Vasant instead, leading his troops. The general who had killed my father in battle and who had injured me to the point I couldn't move a muscle while Vasant killed the royal family.

The one, besides Vasant, I loathed the most.

I gripped the hilt of my sword until my knuckles turned white, fighting the compulsion inside my chest that screamed at me to attack. To get close and stab him in the heart. Plain and simple.

But if I did that, I would be killed two seconds later.

And I wouldn't accomplish my mission.

I inhaled deeply, banishing those murderous thoughts from my mind, and resumed my walk. Thankfully, Xuan finished talking to the soldiers and marched on toward the garrison on the south side.

Holding my breath, I crossed the inner gate.

No one stopped me. I let out a relieved breath as I hurried my steps into the main road of Greentref, the capital of the Spring Court. At this time of the day, the city was bustling. Females with baskets of flowers and bread and fabric, males with carts full of meat, going up and down the streets, entering and exiting shops and houses. Kids ran along the streets, probably on a break from school.

While buried in that dark hole, I had purposely forgotten

all about the Spring Court and what made it so beautiful, so lively, but now that I was up here, watching the smiles, listening to the chatter, smelling the sweet flowers and the pungent spices that made my mouth water and my stomach rumble in protest, staring at the vibrant colors that made up my beloved court, it all came back to me. All my hope, my pride, my will to protect this court rushed back to me and filled my veins.

I had a purpose now, and nothing would stop me.

After a brisk five minute walk, I saw them... the gates of the outer wall. They were bigger and stronger than the inner gates, and harder to get past too. No matter the time of day, those gates remained closed, only allowing authorized fae to come in and out.

My heart thumped fast against my rib cage. I was so, so close to being free, to being able to take the first step that would bring a new future for this land.

My palms sweated as I walked toward it, my brain zooming with excuses. Why would a soldier need to exit the capital alone and by foot in the middle of the day?

Mahaeru's hand was probably at work when the gates opened wide and an old male fae stopped under the archway so the guards could examine his horse and the small cart the animal was pulling. The guards lifted the fabric to check the goods, and I strode forward.

My steps faltered when a soldier stepped out of the outpost beside the gates. Holy petal, it was Hinata, one of the best soldiers under Xuan. What the blossom was he doing here? He wasn't a gate guard.

He knew exactly who I was, but I had Mahaeru's glamour on. He wouldn't recognized me.

Praying for Mahaeru's magic to keep working, I walked

past the guards and the old fae.

But I didn't take two steps past the gates before a hand clasped around my shoulder. "Where are you going?"

I felt the magic falling away, like a cover of water slipping away from me and disappearing into the ground.

Hinata's eyes widened. "Ashton!"

He was so shocked at finding me there, it took him a second to react. By then, I had pulled my sword from its scabbard. I swung it at him, and he jumped back several feet.

The guards forgot about the old fae, his horse, and his cart, instead drawing their swords and pointing them at me.

Holy petal.

Without time to lose, I cut the ropes that tied the horse to the cart, jumped on the horse, and yelled as I kicked the horse's side. The horse shot forward, taking me away from the gates.

Away from Evergreen Castle.

"Hey!" Hinata yelled. He brought his hands high, and vines sprouted under the horse's hooves.

Gritting my teeth, I channeled my still awakening magic and counterattacked his spell by parting the vines before they wrapped around the horse's legs.

Hinata tried again, this time making the vines grow ahead of us. I focused and sent my magic to the earth. It shook, taking the vines back down. The horse faltered with the movement of the ground but didn't stop.

Then we were too far.

Hinata gave up on magic, but I heard him raise the alarm and call for horses.

By the time he started chasing me, I would be miles away.

FOR AN HOUR OR SO, I guided the horse down Glade Road, the main road that cut through the heart of the Spring Court. All I wanted was to get away from the capital.

But that wasn't enough.

I had to find a way to go to Earth and find Eden's daughter. I needed a medallion, but mine had been confiscated long ago. Only royals and high-ranked generals and commanders had the medallions. Why hadn't Mahaeru given me one? She brought my sword, unlocked my chains and my cell, glamoured me, but she couldn't give me one blossoming medallion?

I let out a long sigh.

There was only one option here. I had to go to the Summer Court. I frowned as a new thought came to me. I hadn't had any news while I was in the dungeons. Was Queen Natsia still alive? Was she still queen of the Summer Court? What about the other courts? As I knew well, a lot of things could change in fifteen years.

Eager to leave the Spring Court, I pressed the sides of the horse with my heels, but the animal slowed down. I couldn't blame him. We had been riding for a while. We were both tired and hungry.

In a couple of miles, we would skirt a small village near the border. Despite all the warning bells ringing in my mind, I knew I should stop at the village and get some food—steal it, because Mahaeru hadn't given me any coins either.

But as I approached the village, my heart sank.

Halfway there, the landscape changed. The luscious green grass became brown and dried. The flowers disappeared. The trees seemed dead with rotten trunks and roots. And the village looked more like a stop before Uffern—the underworld. The roads were littered with trash. The usual white and beige paint on the houses was peeling away. The vines along the walls were dead. The brown roofs were broken. The few people in the street were dirty, wearing rags just like I was, and their faces were too thin, their eyes sunken, and their bodies gaunt.

My chest constricted.

I hid the horse among some dead trees and approached the village from the side.

A male fae was seated along the wall of an abandoned shop, his breathing ragged.

I nudged his legs. "Hey." The male fluttered his eyes open, something that seemed to take a lot energy to do. "What happened here?"

The male snorted. "What do you mean? It has been like that for almost fifteen years," the male said, his voice frail.

Fifteen years. Since Vasant took over the crown.

"What happened to the officials of this village?" I asked. "Do you know if they sent reports and complained?"

"Oh, the village's lords sent many reports and complaints," the old male said. "One day, soldiers came to the village, and we thought they were here to address the reports." The male shook his head. "They publicly executed the lords and told us all that if we continued to complain, we would all be executed like that."

I stared at the male, not believing what I was hearing. "That can't be," I whispered.

"But that's exactly what happened. That fake king," the male rasped. "It's forbidden to talk badly about him, but I don't care. That fake king is destroying our court."

"What do you mean? This isn't the only place like this?"

The male shook his head. "Only a handful of towns around the capital are still intact. The rest of the court is just like this." He gestured toward the center of the dying village. "Abandoned. Destroyed. Dead."

I clenched my hands as a new wave of rage made me breathless. I thought I hated Vasant before, but with each passing minute, I hated him more and more. What the blossom had he done to my court?

I tried calming down before I acted rashly. I couldn't hurry up things. I had finally escaped, and I was on my way to put an end to his tyranny, though it would take a while for me to start anything.

Giving up on my idea of stealing food from these fae, I dragged my feet out of the village, mounted the waiting horse, and galloped away.

I RODE the nameless horse for days and days. Since I couldn't go into Niwtrall in the center of Wyth to reach the Summer Court, I had to go through the Dawn Court. It would have been easier if the Dawn Court weren't so neutral and liked to avoid conflicts. Otherwise, I would have asked for their help instead.

I crossed the border and, instead of hiding, went directly to the first outpost. There, I met with a general who I had seen a few times before but thankfully had never fought with.

"I heard you were dead," he said, completely shocked at seeing me standing in front of him. At the outpost, the general let me take a bath, change my clothes, eat a hearthy meal—I licked my fingers and immediately threw up since my stomach wasn't used to real food anymore. The general also gave me a stronger horse, saying I would need it if I were to cross the Dawn Court into Summer.

More importantly, he told me what he knew from after I was captured.

"Most of the Spring soldiers, the ones supporting King Eden, were killed," he said. "Others were captured and tortured until they agreed to join Vasant's army. However, I heard most of them died while being tortured." My stomach twisted in knots. I knew very well how hard it was to survive that. "To tell you the truth, Vasant has been unusually quiet, but from the last I heard, his army has grown exponentially, and they are always training, as if a war would erupt at any time."

If Vasant was planning a new war, who was it against? Hadn't he taken all of the Spring Court? What else did he want?

The general also told me that all supporters of King Eden who had survived the war were publicly executed as a warning to those who decided to oppose Vasant. And, confirming what the elder had told me a few days ago, the general said most of the villages in the Spring Court were ignored, as if only Greentref and a handful others were deemed worthy of attention and care.

Hearing all of this made me more determined to do something, to find Eden's daughter, to get an army together and fight this fake king.

But first, I needed to get to the Summer Court.

I rode for another handful of days until I reached the border of the Dawn Court and the Summer Court. The scenery changed, becoming a vast desert under a baking sun. There, I was immediately recognized and brought to the Sun City, the capital, via one of their sandsailers—a wooden boat of sorts that glided over the sand using magic. It would be faster than a horse.

General Behar met me at the gates of the Sun City. "By the scorching heat, I thought I would never see you again." We clasped forearms, a warrior's greeting. He frowned as he squeezed my arms. "You've lost weight."

I scoffed. "Try staying in a dungeon and eating only moldy bread and water for fifteen years."

I said it lighthearted, but the pain in his eyes triggered the pain I had felt during that long time. After fleeing for days, I was so blooming tired, I didn't think I could stand for another two seconds.

Behar took me to the Summer castle and led me to a guest suite. "There's clean clothes in the closet and food at the table." He pointed to the low table beside the large bed. "I'll be sending a healer to look over you."

"No, Behar, I don't have time for this," I told him. "I need to talk to the queen right now."

Behar shook his head. "She isn't here, Ashton. Queen Natsia and Prince Varian went to a village in the north for a festival. They should arrive here in two days. Meanwhile, I suggest you rest and take care of your health."

I groaned. There was no time for this! I had to find Eden's daughter *now* and bring her back so she could claim the throne. The longer it took me to find her, the longer it would be until the Spring Court was safe from the fake king.

But, without a choice, I nodded.

A HEALER CAME and treated my wounds. He said that all of them would heal fine, but there was nothing he could do about the many scars all over my body. He also prescribed a strong tea to help me sleep at night, since I told him I hadn't slept well in fifteen years.

A young male servant came to cut my long, knotted hair into a shorter, manageable style, shave my thick beard, and trim my sharp nails. He also brought food to my room every few hours. Like before, I threw up right after eating, but it was less and less. I knew soon my stomach would get used to it and I would feel normal again.

And after drinking from the healer's tea, I slept for two days straight. While in the dungeons, I hadn't slept for more than two hours at a time, and every time I closed my eyes, nightmares filled my mind and I woke up feeling worse. With this miraculous tea, I hadn't even dreamed.

General Behar came into my suite and woke me up. "The queen is back. She's waiting for you in her study."

I scrambled off the floor, where I had been sleeping, took a quick bath, changed clothes once again, and followed Behar to the queen's study.

Like the rest of the castle, the study was a large room with sand-colored walls and furniture. Everything in the Summer Court was neutral and simplistic, aside from some decorations that screamed with colors—most of them yellow and gold with a splash of light green and blue. The floor was a rough stone, and there were round pillars on the sides of the room, just like in many rooms of the palace.

The queen stood behind the long desk, wearing a beige dress and her golden crown firmly atop her dark hair, which had been pulled into a low bun. Prince Varian stood beside the desk, looking regal as always in a beige suit. His long, brown hair was secured in a ponytail behind his back.

"By the scorching sun, General Ashton," the queen said, sounding amazed. "I can't believe my eyes. Is that really you?"

"Queen Natsia, Prince Varian." I bowed my head to both. "It's an immense pleasure to be able to see you both again."

"After all you went through, you must be tired," Prince Varian said. He gestured to one of the armchairs before the queen's desk. "Please, sit down." He glanced to Behar. "Please have a maid bring food and drinks."

Behar bowed and exited the room.

I took the seat, not because I was tired, but I didn't want to go against the prince of the Summer Court.

"I imagine you also want refuge," the queen said. Queen Natsia was known for getting directly to the point.

I frowned. "What do you mean also?"

She and Varian shared a glance. "You probably don't know," the queen said, her voice low. "Princess Mae, Prince Mallow, and Princess Tansy live here with us."

I blinked. "W-What?"

Princess Petal and Princess Mae were King Eden's and Vasant's sisters. Princess Tansy was Petal's daughter, and Prince Mallow was Mae's son. It had been Petal who had opened the gates and allowed Vasant to enter the Evergreen Palace that terrible day. In the end, Vasant had killed not only King Eden, Queen Elowen, Prince Wells, and Princess Ayla, but also Princess Petal—the very one who had helped him.

I thought all the others had perished too.

I didn't understand. If Princess Mae, Prince Mallow, and Princess Tansy were alive, why were they hiding here?

"Princess Tansy is very sorry for her mother's act," the queen continued. "She has become one of the priestesses of the Moon Temple here at the palace."

"As for Princess Mae and Prince Mallow, they said they tried to help, but when Vasant turned to them, they ran," Prince Varian said. "Princess Mae lives in a small cottage behind the castle, and Prince Mallow married a lady from a noble family here in the Summer Court."

I stared at the queen. "They have no interest in the terrors afflicting their own court?"

"I'm afraid they don't consider the Spring Court their own anymore," she said, her tone heartfelt. "I also know they are scared of Vasant. He has become a crazy fae, hungry for power." She tsked. "Just a few months ago, he humiliated King Cadewyn's mate. Cadewyn was furious, of course, but thankfully, he didn't start another war." She let out a long sigh. "Though I've heard Vasant has been growing his army more and more. My spies tell me it seems he's preparing for a war."

"Spies?" I asked, confused.

"Oh, yes, after all that happened, I sent spies to the Spring Court," the queen confessed. "If Vasant turns against the rest of Wyth, I want to be the first to know."

"Though, the lives of our spies haven't been easy," Prince Varian added. "A few were caught and killed, and others are having difficulty infiltrating their ranks."

The queen frowned. "But tell me, how did you escape?"

"Mahaeru helped me," I told them.

"What?" the queen asked, shocked. "The goddess helped you?"

I nodded. "She told me it was time to finish my king's last mission."

"Which is?" Prince Varian asked.

"A few months before being killed, King Eden told me he had another child, a half human who he had sent back to Earth with her mother to keep safe. He said that if anything happened to him and his heirs, I should wait until she was of age and bring her back so she could claim the throne."

Prince Varian sucked in a sharp breath. "You're talking about reigniting the war here."

My hands curled into fists as my chest filled with rage for the man who had destroyed my court. "If that's what it takes to get the throne back from the fake king, I don't care."

The queen and the prince exchanged a meaningful glance.

"General Ashton, I'll be frank," the queen said, as if she had never been. "We have no desire to participate in a war. Our kingdom is living harmoniously, and I don't plan on changing that. But... I can help you by giving you supplies and a medallion so you can go find Eden's daughter. No more than that."

I knew that, but deep down I had hoped they would tell me they would stand by my side and help me take the Spring Court back. I let out a long breath. "I understand."

The queen opened a drawer on her desk and picked up a medallion. She offered it to me. "Here it is. You can keep it."

I took it from her and cradled it in my hands as if it were the most precious thing I had ever owned. "Thank you." I paused, thinking. "Before I go, can I send a message to some friends?"

Prince Varian frowned. "Are you sure you can trust them?"

I nodded. "I have always trusted them with my life. I'm sure that, if they are still alive, they will come to my aid."

"Then write your messages," Prince Varian said. "I'll make sure they are sent safely."

"Thank you."

I was given paper and ink, and quickly wrote down the short notes to my soldiers. Then I used the medallion and went to Earth to find Eden's daughter.

I TURNED OFF THE LIGHTS, closed and locked the doors, and turned away from the shop. Usually, we closed the store at six in the evening, but sometimes on Fridays, we had more orders than usual, and I always spent one or two more hours trying to get everything done.

This evening, I didn't have much to do, so I sent my mother ahead to cook us some dinner—I hadn't eaten since lunch and I was starving.

With my purse slung across my shoulders, I started my walk home. Our small house was in a simple subdivision, just five blocks from the store, which made the commute convenient. If it were up to me, I'd always come to work on foot, but because we had so many deliveries, my mother insisted we drive the car.

I looked up at the sky. It was almost eight at night. At this time of the year, the sun was just now disappearing on the horizon, and the sky was a splash of colors—orange, pink, dark blue. It reminded me of a beautiful painting, which would look fabulous hanging on a wall flanked by vases with flowers of the same colors.

I smiled, amazed that my mind always went there—flowers and plants and green, lots and lots of green.

Perhaps my next vacation should be a small cabin in the mountains, not at the beach. I let out a sigh. Peter had come to the shop once more earlier this week, and I almost threw a vase at his head. That night, Sarah had called to tell me her spring break had just started and she was having loads of fun. For a moment there, I almost dropped everything and joined her.

But I didn't. I was happy here, with the shop and my mother. I didn't need to party all night and drink until I passed out. Besides, I had a big project to work on for my economics class. I had already started it, and my plan was to finish it by Sunday, way ahead of schedule.

Two blocks into my journey, a shiver rolled down my spine.

I stiffened. What the hell was that?

I glanced back. Was there someone following me? I didn't see anyone, but I had this feeling like I was being watched.

Despite the logical part of my brain telling me that Greendale was a nice, quiet town, I sped up, suddenly eager to get home.

For the next three blocks, the feeling didn't leave me. In fact, it only became more powerful. By the last half block, I was practically jogging.

I hurried inside the house and locked the door. I rested my back against the wall and took a deep breath.

My mother stepped out of the kitchen with a smile. "Right on time. Dinner is ready." She saw me and frowned. "Something wrong?"

"I...." I shook my head. This was ridiculous. What could I tell her? That I had been followed? Why me? I wasn't pretty enough for a creep to be obsessed with me, and I wasn't rich enough to be robbed. I took a long, calming breath. "It's nothing. Let's go eat."

The doorbell rang, and I let out a yelp.

My mother stared at me as if I were crazy. Then she turned her gaze to the door. We usually didn't have any visitors, much less late at night. Slowly, my mother went to the door and looked out of the thin side window.

She pulled back, her face white. I thought she would tell me to call 911 or something, but then she opened the door and stared at the man standing on the porch. "General Ashton."

My brows curled down as I took in the man. The first things I noticed was that he was tall and wide, and his arms and shoulders barely fit in the leather jacket he was wearing. The green T-shirt underneath hugged his torso, showing off his sculpted chest and his six-pack. The guy was ripped as hell. But besides being hot, he was handsome. His hair was sandy blonde, his eyes bright green, and the sharp angles of his face screamed masculinity. If I hadn't known better, I would say this man was a freaking underwear model.

What was he doing at my house?

More importantly, how did my mother know him?

The man bowed his head to me before greeting my mother. "Hello, Amelia."

My mother stepped back. "Come in, please." The big man entered our house, and my mother closed the door. "May I ask you what brings you here?"

The man started talking, but I didn't understand a single word. The words seemed like gibberish, but with a musical intonation to them. I stared at him, who seemed to be a lunatic, and my mother, who was equally crazy, because she nodded as if she understood him.

I gasped when my mother replied in the same kind of gibberish the man had spoken.

"What the hell is going on?" I asked, confused.

My mother turned to me, her eyes downcast. "I... I'll take him to the guest bedroom; then I'll come back so we can talk about this."

"Wait, what?" I pointed to the man. "You're letting this stranger spend the night here?"

"He's not a stranger, Hayley," my mother said, sounding sad. "And he has been through a lot. Let me get him settled. Then I'll come back to talk to you."

I opened my mouth to protest some more, but my mother simply marched past me, the man following her. They went upstairs, talking in that strange language.

I stayed planted in place, not believing what had just happened here.

Suddenly, my hunger was gone. All I wanted was answers.

WHEN AMELIA OPENED the door and I saw Eden's daughter in full light, my heart stopped.

This was she. This was my queen.

And she was breathtaking. With her long, blonde hair, her fair skin, her sea-green eyes, and her delicate features, there was no denying she was a Spring Court half-fae. All that was missing was the pointed ears, but I knew those would come out soon.

In fae language, I explained to Amelia all that had happened since she left with Hayley—the continuation of the war, the betrayal, King Eden's death, his family's demise, my imprisonment. I even told her that Mahaeru had been the one who freed me. Amelia might be human, but she had lived in the Spring Court for a long time and she knew all about the fae, including the importance of the goddesses. If Mahaeru had a hand in sending me here, then this was important.

"I haven't told Hayley anything," Amelia told me, her voice almost breaking. She had aged since I had last seen her, but she was still a beautiful woman. "She doesn't know about her father, about magic, about Wyth. Let me tell her. Alone."

Though I knew it would take over a day, or a month, to take back the throne of the Spring Court, I didn't want to waste time. I wanted to go back to Wyth *now*. The sooner we started this blooming war, the sooner it would be over.

I could give Amelia a couple of hours to talk to her daughter alone, though.

So I followed Amelia to the second floor of the small but quaint house. On our way, I checked everything. The doors, how many windows there were, if they were of easy access, what was behind the house. Though I didn't think anyone else knew about Eden's daughter, I felt like I had to do anything and everything to keep her safe. After all, this was my queen.

I retreated to the guest bedroom, but I didn't stay there. Once Amelia went back downstairs, I exited the room and halted atop of the stairs, where I could see Amelia's back as she stopped in front of Hayley in the living room.

"You better sit down for this conversation," Amelia said in their language. I could understand almost everything, but my tongue still twisted when I tried speaking it. Besides, it had been over fifteen years since I had practiced it. I was just grateful I could still understand most of it.

Hayley crossed her arms. "Just tell me what is going on."

I stared at the future queen of the Spring Court, mesmerized. Besides beautiful, she was fierce. She looked like she could take on the world with that defiance.

A warmth started deep in my chest, and I felt rather proud. I had found her. I had found my queen.

Amelia let out a long sigh. "Your father's name is Eden.

He was the king of the Spring Court in Wyth, a continent in the fae realm. And—"

Laughter bubbled out of Hayley's lips. "Are you freaking joking?"

Her mother shook her head. "I'm telling you the truth. My great-grandparents were changelings—humans who had been traded by fae and brought to Wyth to be slaves. Though, by the time my grandparents were born, the Spring Court abolished the changeling exchange. Some humans chose to come back to Earth, but not my grandparents. They became servants in the Evergreen Palace, the castle in the Spring Court. I grew up free, but being a human among fae isn't easy. Though, I was lucky. I could sing. I became a singer for the royal family. And... I fell in love with the king." Amelia paused and wiped her face. "And the king fell in love with me. We had an affair, and that's how you came to be."

Hayley lifted a finger. "Affair? As in... he was married?"

Amelia nodded. "I'm not proud of that, but once the heart is set, it's hard to stop. Though, in my defense, Queen Elowen wasn't Eden's mate. As far as I know, they didn't love each other. They had an arranged marriage to produce heirs."

Hayley shook her head. "This is all nonsense."

"I know how you must feel. I know it all sounds crazy, but it's the truth," Amelia said, her tone pleading. "There was a big war in the Spring Court when I fell in love, but for a while, it seemed contained. Then you were born, and Eden was afraid you could be used against him." That wasn't the entire truth. When the king told me about this secret, he also said that he wasn't just protecting Hayley and Amelia from the war, but from Queen Elowen too. The queen was a fair woman, but she could be too practical sometimes. King Eden was afraid the queen would hurt Amelia and Hayley if she found out about them. Or worse. "So he sent us back to Earth," Amelia continued. "He told us to come and move to a town he didn't know, that no one knew, so if someone found out about us, it would be harder for them to actually find us."

Hayley pointed up. "Clearly, it wasn't that hard to find us."

It had been, to some extent. I had been on Earth for three days already and had just found them.

"General Ashton is... was the best warrior in the Spring Court," Amelia said. I didn't like the *was* in her sentence, but it was true. After fifteen years locked away, I had lost most of my mass and power, and I was probably very rusty. "If anyone can find us, it's him. Anyway, he came here to tell us that the war went on after we left, and that your father and his entire family were killed fifteen years ago."

Hayley sat down on the couch. "I... I don't know." She pressed her hand to her chest. "Why am I feeling like this when all you're saying is just nuts?"

"Because it's true." Amelia sat down beside her. "Vasant, Eden's younger brother, was the one behind the war. He was the one who killed Eden and everyone else. Then he took the throne for himself."

Hayley frowned. "The king's brother. It is a sad story, but he has royal blood too."

"True, but Vasant is wicked. I never liked him before, and now... now I loathe him." Amelia's voice trembled with emotion. "General Ashton told me he's destroying the Spring Court. And even though he already stole the crown, he's still growing his army. Ashton thinks he'll start attacking other courts soon."

"Mom... this is nuts. Are you hearing yourself?" Hayley took her mother's hands in hers. "What you're saying, it doesn't make any sense."

"Didn't you just feel sad when I told you that your father was assassinated? What was that if you don't believe me?"

Hayley opened and closed her mouth. "I.... It was just me reacting to a sob story. I would cry for a homeless man if you told me his entire family was killed unjustly."

"Hayley, please, sweetheart." Amelia closed her eyes for a moment. "I know it sounds crazy, I know. But it's not. You're half-fae and you're heir to the throne."

Hayley's mouth fell open. "W-What?"

"That's why Ashton is here," Amelia continued. "He wants to take you to the Spring Court, so you can help him get an army and fight Vasant. He wants you to steal the throne back."

"What?" Hayley shot to her feet. "I'm not going anywhere."

Her mother stood alongside her. "I agree. I understand how things turned out and why you would be the best solution right now, but it's too dangerous. I don't want that for you. But we can't tell Ashton that. He's a warrior, and he's going to flip if we just tell him you won't go."

The desire to storm down the stairs and confront them hit me hard, but I clenched my hands into fists and held back.

Like Amelia had said, I had to give Hayley time to absorb all of this information. But I wouldn't flip on them if Hayley told me she wouldn't come with me.

I would simply take her by force.

WHILE MY MOTHER explained to me about my father, fae, and the Spring Court, all I could think was that she had been reading too many fantasy novels.

Seriously? Me being a half-fae and heir to the throne of a fantasy land located in some other realm? That was a bit of a stretch.

Oh, shit, what if my mother was losing it? What if she was having some early-onset Alzheimer's or something like that, and this delusion was part of it? I couldn't deal with my mother being sick like that. She was too young, and she was the only one I had.

If something happened to her....

I sucked in a sharp breath and turned to the mirror over the dresser in my bedroom. I stared into my own eyes. Half-fae. How could that be? I was plain human.

I glanced at the closed bedroom door. I had locked it when I came in after talking to my mother—as if I would leave it open with a stranger just across the hall.

After my mother told me Ashton was here to take me to

the Spring Court, I told her to stop. I didn't want to hear her nonsense anymore. I hoped that a good night's sleep would actually make all the difference and tomorrow she would wake up saying she was playing a joke on me.

I rubbed my hand over my chest. Why was this damn feeling stinging inside me? This sadness, this heavy gloom that made no sense.

After changing into my pajamas, I turned off the light and lay down in my bed. But sleep didn't come. How could I sleep after all the craziness my mother told me? I was seriously worried about her. But more importantly, I was conscious of the big man sleeping across the hallway.

I didn't like having him here, and I was hoping that tomorrow morning my mother would tell him to leave.

A faint creak came from the other side of my door. Then a little rumble.

I sat up in bed. What the hell was going on? When the creaking sound came again, I hopped out of the bed. Was the stranger tiptoeing outside or going down the stairs? With slow steps, I crept to my door. I placed my ear on the wood, straining my ears, but all I heard was the creaking sound followed by the faint rumbling.

If this were a horror movie, these noises would signal the incoming of a horrible death. Mine, in this case. But as I refused to believe in fae, I refused to believe that I would die like that. So I grabbed my long gray robe from the hook on the wall, put it on, opened the door a tiny crack, and peeked out.

The creaking echoed through the hallway, louder this time. I flung my door open and looked to both sides. Moon-light streamed in the hallway from the window above the stairs, illuminating just enough. There was nothing there.

The sound came again, followed not by rumbling, but a whimper.

It was coming from the guest bedroom.

I stared at the closed door. What the hell was going on?

A louder whimper pushed me to move. I knocked on the door, careful not to wake up my mother—she was a heavy sleeper, but even she would wake up if I went around banging on doors.

"Ashton?" I called out, my voice low. "Everything okay?"

He didn't answer, though he whimpered again.

I stepped back. He was probably having a nightmare. I shouldn't go into the bedroom in the middle of the night because of that. I took another step back when a louder creak and a grunt came from inside the room.

Shit.

Feeling like a creep, I opened the door of the guest bedroom and started inside. For a moment, I was confused. There was no one in the bed.

Then I heard him. Lying on the carpet beside the bed, Ashton tossed and turned, his face wrinkled as if he were in pain. He whimpered again, his arms jerking.

Whatever this nightmare was, it wasn't good.

"Ashton?" I called as I knelt beside him. "Ashton, wake up." I shook his shoulder.

The moment my hand touched him, Ashton's eyes shot open. In one fluid motion, he grabbed both my wrists and flipped us, pinning me against the floor under him. He bared his teeth and growled.

Then his eyes went wide as he stared at me.

For a moment, he was frozen.

I stared at him, my heart thumping hard against my chest

with the scare of being thrown to the floor but also from having a man over me like that.

It had been a while since I had been with anyone, and having this big man holding me down was exciting. I shook my head, thinking I had gone crazy too. Shit, how could I think of that right now? But how could I not when he was wearing nothing but sweatpants. It was dark in the bedroom, but I could make out the hundreds of muscles covering his shoulders, arms, chest, and stomach.

I swallowed hard.

Ashton jumped back and away from me. On his knees, he lowered his head. "My queen, I'm sorry. I'm so, so sorry."

Frowning, I sat up. "It's okay. I probably startled you."

"That is no excuse, my queen," he said, his English a little broken and his accent rich and deep. "I should be punishment for that, my queen."

With a sigh, I rose to my feet. "First of all, stop this 'my queen' nonsense. It's getting on my nerves. Second, it's okay. No need for punishment. Just go back to sleep."

I hurried out of the bedroom, not sure why. Had I been afraid of him? No. Had I been afraid of my reaction to him? Yes. Definitely, yes.

Suddenly feeling a little hot and parched, I went downstairs to the kitchen, where I turned on the lights and grabbed a glass full of cold water. I sat down on one of kitchen counter's stools and stared at the clock on the microwave.

It wasn't even midnight, and I already knew this night would be shitty. There was no way I could sleep tonight, for several reasons.

Not five minutes later, Ashton joined me in the kitchen.

At least now he was wearing a loose T-shirt. But once

more he lowered his head. "My queen, I want to apologize again."

"Ashton, I already told you. Stop calling me 'my queen.' I'm not your queen, and I won't be your queen."

Ashton faced me, his eyes wide for a second. "What could I say to change your mind?"

"First, you should stop with this fae and queen thing, or I'll kick you out of this house, even if you are a guest of my mother's. Second, if my mother insists on the same topic, I'll take her to a doctor or a shrink, whoever can see her first." I shook my head. "You two sound way too crazy. I can't be the only sane person here."

"I not crazy, my qu—" I shot him a glare, and he closed his mouth, swallowing his words. "I'm not crazy. If you come with me, I'll prove it to you."

I snorted. Did he really think I would go anywhere with him? Did I look that stupid?

"Nobody can sleep, hm?" My mother walked into the kitchen. She offered us a small smile. "I certainly can't."

I drank a long swallow of water. "Well, since we are all up, how about if we talk about all this shit you told me earlier?" Not that I wanted to, but we needed to clear the air. They had to stop this bullshit right now. Ashton turned to my mother and said something in that odd language. I pointed to him. "And stop talking that damned language!"

Ashton bowed his head. "As you wish, my queen."

"Holy shit," I snapped, annoyed with him.

"Hayley," my mother called me, her voice sweet. "Please, calm down."

"Calm down? Calm down?" I jumped from the stool and started pacing around the kitchen. "You're talking in a strange language that sounds like pure gibberish, and you're telling me stories that sound like fairy tales straight from a book. Then this guy," I gestured to Ashton, "shows up out of nowhere and is now calling me queen. How can I freaking calm down?"

"I know it sounds—"

"Shh," Ashton said, cutting my mother off. He put a finger over his lips. "I hear something."

I rolled my eyes. What now?

Then the back door blew open with a loud thud and a man barged in. I went completely still as he pointed his weapon at me and spoke in that strange language.

Ashton grabbed my wrist and pulled me behind him. "Over my dead body."

THE MOMENT the Spring Court soldier stormed into the house with his dark green and golden uniform and pointing the golden blade of his spear at Hayley's head, my blood turned cold.

A sliver of panic snaked through my chest.

No, not my queen.

I tugged Hayley behind me and faced the soldier, cursing myself for leaving my sword upstairs. Holy petal, they had found Hayley but how?

"General Ashton, step aside if you don't want to die," the soldier said, the golden blade of his spear trained on the middle of my chest.

"Over my dead body," I said in English, because my queen had asked me to stop speaking fae.

Three more soldiers stepped through the door. I retreated two feet, taking Hayley with me. Her mother scurried back, hiding behind me with Hayley.

I watched the soldiers. Four. For some reason, I was sure there were more soldiers outside. Panic threatened to seize my chest. I hadn't fought anyone in almost fifteen years, which meant I was rusty. I'd also lost strength and muscle mass while locked in the dungeons, and my sword was currently glamoured and out of reach. I wondered if I'd be able to win this fight.

No, no time to wonder. I had to believe I could. That I would. My queen's life and the future of the Spring Court depended on it.

"Your loss, General." The first soldier advanced.

I reached for a knife on the kitchen counter and swiped it wide as the soldier came at us with his spear. The knife hit the blade of the spear, shaking my arm hard with incredible force.

Behind me, Hayley yelped.

No, I wouldn't let my queen be afraid.

I channeled my magic. It filled my veins, warming my body. I inhaled deeply, welcoming it, like a junkie who had been without his drugs for so long. I had missed this feeling. I had missed this power.

I threw my hand toward the plant in the corner of the kitchen, sending my magic to it. Instantly, the plant grew and its branches extended, becoming long vines. It wrapped around the four soldiers.

But they had the same magic as me. They started breaking the vines away. I didn't waste time. While they were busy undoing my spell, I stepped forward and plunged the knife in the chest of one soldier and slashed the throat of another.

Their bodies fell at my feet, their blood staining the wooden floor.

The other two, now free from the vines, bared their teeth at us, their spears pointed high.

Kicking up one of the spears from the floor, I grabbed it and positioned myself for a real fight, my feet braced apart. The two soldiers ran toward me. I threw the spear at one's chest, then spun around, grabbed the other spear from the floor, and pierced the fourth soldier's side. His step faltered, and he dropped his weapon.

I called on my magic again. Once more, the plant grew and its branches extended, wrapping around the soldier's torso. I sent as much of my power as I could, fighting his magic as he tried to break free. I placed the tip of the spear's blade over his chest.

"Why are you here?" I asked in fae, pressing the blade into his skin.

The soldier laughed, showing off his bloodstained teeth. "King Vasant never stopped trying to eliminate any ties that pointed back to Eden." He shifted his gaze to the women behind me. "He sent us to kill Eden's daughter."

"How did he know?"

I didn't expect the soldier to answer, but he laughed again before telling me. "King Vasant finally found and interviewed an old fae who worked at the palace a couple of months ago. She told him that Eden was very fond of his musicians. So King Vasant went after the musicians. One of them told him that Eden had had an affair with a human female named Amelia and that Amelia had a daughter. Then one day both of them suddenly disappeared." He licked his lips. "He sent us here to find them."

I pressed the blade to his chest more firmly. "What does Vasant want with them?"

The soldier groaned but chuckled again. "What do you think? He wants to kill Eden's daughter."

I had thought as much, but it was one thing to think it,

another to know it. Vasant wanted to kill her so she couldn't claim the throne.

I wouldn't let that happen.

"How many more are outside?"

"Too many for you to fight alone," the soldier said, spitting blood with each of his words. He was dying, probably suffering.

Hating this part of the job, I gritted my teeth and plunged the spear into his chest.

The soldier gasped. A moment later, his eyes rolled back. I dropped the magic on the vines, unwrapping them from around him. His body fell with the others.

Holding the spear, I turned to Hayley and Amelia. "Are you okay?" I asked in English.

Hands around her daughter and her eyes wide, Amelia nodded. Beside her, Hayley was too pale and her arms shook slightly.

"You...." She fixed those pretty sea-green eyes on mine. "You killed these men."

"Spring Court soldiers," I explained. "They were sent here to kill you." I looked at Amelia and continued in fae since trying to speak English all the time was giving me a headache. "There are more soldiers outside. Break the spell binding her."

"H-How do you know about that?" Amelia asked.

"I can feel it," I said, though I had no idea how I could feel it. But now that my own powers were running under my skin, I could sense Hayley's powers locked inside of her. "Break the spell. She'll be able to see through their glamour. She'll know they aren't simply men. And she'll be able to understand us."

More importantly, she would be able to use her magic to defend herself, if it came to that. Even if she had no idea how to use it, I bet that on instinct, she could at least wrap some vines around her enemy or shake the ground and make them unstable.

A loud snapping sound came from outside.

"What was that?" Hayley asked, holding on to her mother's arms.

"Amelia, please, do it," I pleaded, knowing we didn't have much time.

Amelia pursed her lips as she glanced at Hayley.

"What's going on?" Hayley asked as her mother slipped a simple iron ring from her finger.

Iron. A metal that could kill fae. Clever.

Amelia closed her hand around the ring. "This isn't what I wanted for you, sweetheart, but now that they found you, they won't stop. I'm sorry." She placed the ring on the kitchen counter, grabbed a metal hammer of sorts from one of drawers, and crushed the ring with it.

Hayley gasped as her power awoke and coursed through her body—such intense and unruly magic that brushed against my skin and made me shiver. Now, she should have the sight and the speech. She could see the pointed ears of the soldiers on the floor, and if I spoke, she would understand me.

"What is happening to me?" she asked, her voice faint. With wide eyes, she watched her hands, as if she could see the magic inside her.

I opened my mouth to explain to her, but before I could, more fae rushed into the house—six of them. Holy petal, how many had come to kill my queen?

I twirled the spear in my hand and turned to them, keeping Hayley and her mother at my back. "You're all dead," I snarled at them.

This time, I didn't wait for them to attack. I rushed at them first. In less than ten seconds, I had two of them writhing on the ground. Perhaps I wasn't as rusty as I first thought, though I knew if we got out of here—when—I would be hurting all over.

A loud bang came from behind me.

I snapped my head in that direction.

The front door was pushed open so hard it fell off the hinges, and another four soldiers marched in the house.

No, no, no.

Distracted, I let my guard down, and the soldier in front of me slashed his blade across my upper arm. I hissed in pain.

Without wasting time, I grabbed his spear just below the blade and pushed it aside, giving me an opening. Then I stabbed him with my spear.

I didn't wait to take the spear out or watch his body fall. No, I just turned and sprinted toward Hayley.

But I was too late.

One of the soldiers across the house lifted his hand, aimed his spear, and threw it at Hayley.

"No!" Amelia shouted.

She stepped in front of Hayley.

The spear plunged into Amelia's chest.

I STARED AT MY MOTHER, at how she kneeled on the floor just a foot from me, at how the weapon stuck from her chest, at how blood seeped from the wound, soaking her pajamas and creating a pool around her.

"No, no, no," I whispered, kneeling beside her. I held on to her shoulders, trying to touch her, to hold her, but not mess with that freaking spear in her chest. Her body convulsed, and I helped her lie down on the floor. "Mom, please, hang on." I brushed her hair from her face as tears brimmed in my eyes. I glanced around, searching for my phone, but I left it upstairs. I had to call 911 right now. "Mom, I'll grab my phone upstairs. Hang on."

I started pushing up from the floor, but she reached up and wrapped her hand around my wrist. "T-There's no time," she croaked, her voice low. "Just... stay with the general. He'll protect you."

A tear escaped and rolled down my cheek. "Don't talk like that. Everything will be fine."

"With him, you'll be fine." She grunted. Her eyes rolled back, and her hand fell from my wrist.

I stared at her in complete shock.

No, no, this had to be a dream. A nightmare. That was it. I had gone to sleep and dreamed about all this fae nonsense, and now I was having a terrible nightmare. I would soon wake up and find all these fae gone, my house pristine, and my mother making us breakfast.

I shut my eyes tight.

The noise of clanking metal and grunts reached my ears. It wasn't a nightmare. Ashton was just beside me, fighting to keep the soldiers from killing me too.

Just like they had killed my mother.

A sob ripped from my throat. My sorrow and panic flared inside me, and I screamed.

Suddenly, the house shook. Vines broke through the floorboards and wound around all of the fae in the house, including Ashton.

Wiping the tears away from my face, I stood and faced them. There were seven fae still standing, all of them jerking against the vines but unable to break through. I knew I had conjured the vines, but I had no idea how.

"Let me go, my queen, so I can help you," Ashton said in fae language. It should surprise me that I understood him, but right then, I was too overwhelmed with my feelings to care about something so insignificant.

I clenched my fists, and the vines tightened around them all. "Why? Why should I let you go? It's your fault all of this happened. If you hadn't come, the soldiers wouldn't have found us."

Ashton groaned. "That's not true. They knew about you. They came for you."

I snorted. "So you're saying it's a coincidence?"

"No, I'm saying that's why Mahaeru, one of the goddesses of Wyth, helped me escape and come to you. So I could be here when they came, so I could protect you."

I gestured to my mother's body at my feet. "Does this look like you're doing a good job?" Another sob choked me, and I felt like crumbling to the floor, curling into a fetal position, and never getting up.

"My queen—"

"DON'T CALL ME THAT!"

Ashton closed his eyes for a moment. "Hayley," he said, his voice thick, as if my name disgusted him. "Soon, the soldiers will be able to break through your magic." I glanced around. The soldiers jerked against the vines, pushing against whatever I was doing to keep them there. I honestly had no idea what I was doing. I was just channeling my anger, my sorrow, and letting it all out. "They are here for you. If you don't let me save you, they will kill you."

One of the soldiers roared, startling me. He lurched against the vines. In my shock, the feeling that was keeping this power up faded, and the vines loosened. He got free and aimed his spear at me.

"Hayley!" Ashton cried. He disentangled himself from the vines and rushed to me, pushing me away as he engaged with the coming soldier.

Ashton grabbed the vines I had brought up inside the house and wound them around the soldier's spear, forcing it to the floor. His attacker let go of the spear and raised his arms for a fist fight, but Ashton was faster. He landed a strong punch on the soldier's nose, sending him staggering back-ward. Then he grabbed the spear from the floor and turned to the other six fae, who were all free by now.

I closed my eyes, not believing any of this.

No, there weren't men with pointed ears in my kitchen.

No, there weren't vines breaking through the floorboards of my house.

No, my mother's body wasn't lifeless at my feet.

Not caring about anything else, I knelt beside my mother. I brushed the hair from her face and pretended she was only sleeping. I pretended I didn't hear the loud noises of metal clashing and the grunts coming from behind me. I pretended I was having the worst nightmare of my life.

Minutes later, a body fell beside me, missing my lap by only a couple of inches. I yelped as the fae's eyes stared at me, though they couldn't see anymore.

Bile rose to my throat.

"Are you okay, my queen?" Ashton asked in his own language.

The anger had faded from my veins along with the magic, leaving only devastation and exhaustion in its wake. I didn't have the energy to ask him to stop calling me *my queen* again.

"I don't think so," I confessed in a small voice. I glanced over my shoulder. A sea of bodies and blood covered the kitchen, and Ashton stood in the center, his arms and face just as bloodied.

He watched the door and windows. "I think we're safe for now." He turned his green eyes to me. "But we can't stay here."

I didn't move while he went around the house, doing only heavens knew what. I just stayed beside my mother, caressing her face, taking care of her as if she had a bad cold and needed me to make her some hot chicken soup.

Suddenly, Ashton crouched down beside me. "My queen, we need to go."

"I don't have anywhere to go," I mumbled, my mind numb.

"We still need to go." Ashton clutched my hand in his and tugged me up with him. "I know you're suffering right now, but we can't stay here. More soldiers will be sent soon, and I can't guarantee I'll be able to keep you safe here for long."

He pulled me to the small half bath downstairs and pushed me inside. "Wash up and change." He handed me a duffel bag, one that had been tucked away in my closet.

I peeked inside. There were several of my tees and jeans and bras and undies in here. "What is this?"

"We can't leave with you like that." He gestured to me.

Damn it, I was wearing my pajamas and robe. And my hands were stained red with blood. My stomach turned, and I thought I would spill my guts.

With automatic movements, I closed the door of the half bath and did as instructed. I washed my face and hands and changed into a tee and shorts.

When I exited the half bath, I saw Ashton crouch down and take my mother's body in his arms. Carrying her, he walked outside. My feet moved of their own accord, and I found myself following him. Ashton deposited her on the back seat of her beaten-up sedan, then helped me to the passenger seat. He took the bag from me and threw it in the trunk, along with a long, green sword.

Without a word, he slipped behind the wheel and backed away from our driveway. I stared at my house, sure I wouldn't ever see it again.

As we drove away from my queen's house, a number of thoughts flooded my mind. The first one was that I hadn't been in the human world in many decades. I was amazed I still knew how to drive.

Then my thoughts shifted to Hayley and everything that had just happened. It hadn't been a coincidence I had come for her when I did. I was convinced Mahaeru had sent me here because she knew Vasant had learned about Hayley and had sent his soldiers to find her and kill her.

Once the soldiers didn't return with the news that they had succeeded, Vasant would send more, and I had barely been able to hold my own against these. I wasn't sure I could take much more.

If Hayley hadn't tapped into her powers, I was sure I would have failed in my mission. I almost did, and I had failed my queen by letting her mother die.

I glanced to the passenger seat. Leaned against the seat, Hayley had her eyes closed. Quiet tears spilled down her cheeks, and her lips trembled.

For leaves' sake, how I wanted to reach over and wipe those tears away and promise her nothing like that would ever happen again.

But she was my queen. She had royal blood in her veins. I shouldn't touch her unless it was to get her out of harm's way, and even then it was supposed to be brief. The itch under my skin asking me to forget that rule was hard to refuse. Ever since the moment my eyes first locked on her, I had been drawn to her. A pull like I had never felt before came from deep inside my chest. I believed it was my sense of duty waking up. I hadn't dreamed of ever escaping that dungeon, but here I was, with my queen, fleeing so I could protect her.

So I could take her to the Spring Court.

The thought of just taking her to Wyth against her will crossed my mind one too many times, but it wasn't right. She was my queen, after all. She was the one supposed to be calling the shots.

After just driving aimlessly for a few hours, I stopped the car just off the road, beside a long bridge over a low river. I picked up Amelia's body from the back seat and brought it to the river's bank.

Looking tipsy, Hayley followed me.

With the car's light shining over us, I lowered her mother's body to the ground, where the sandy bank turned into green grass, and channeled my magic. Besides being able to manipulate any plants, I was one of the few fae who could move the earth. That was a rare and coveted power.

I opened my arms, and the earth shook, opening a long, deep hole in the ground.

Realization of what was happening washed over Hayley. Her eyes widened. "What the hell are you doing?"

"Giving her a proper burial," I calmly stated. I understood

she might be upset about where this was headed, but unfortunately, we couldn't keep going with a body on the back seat. We couldn't lug it to the Spring Court and carry it with us during the war. "She'll be honored and accepted with the gods."

Hayley stared in shock as I lowered her mother's body in the hole.

"No, wait." She knelt beside the hole and reached inside, brushing her mother's hand. "I'm not ready for this. Not yet."

I gave her another minute while tears rolled down her face. Then I gently grabbed her shoulders and pulled her back. "I'm sorry, my queen, but it's time."

Hayley lowered her head and quietly sobbed as I called on the vines. I wrapped the vines tightly around the body, covering every inch, and infused some magic on them. Hopefully, this would work and the body would remain intact. Once we won the war and Hayley became the queen, we could come back and take the body to Wyth.

Using my magic, I closed the hole, covering Amelia's body with dirt.

A loud sob cut through Hayley's throat, shaking her shoulders. I let out a long breath, feeling guilt for not being able to protect her mother, while also fighting with my self-control. It wouldn't be right to embrace my queen and comfort her, even in a moment like this.

So I just stood back and watched as my queen suffered.

AFTER THE BURIAL, Hayley acted like a mindless doll. As much as I wanted to respect her grieving, we couldn't stay out in the open like for long, so I carted her to the car and continued driving without direction.

A few minutes into our trip, I glanced at Hayley and found her head lolled back on the seat, her eyes closed, her breathing steady. She was sleeping.

I just kept driving as the sun rose on our backs and slowly started its way up the sky. Back in Wyth, the sun and moon changed colors according to each court, but the Spring Court's sun was very much like the one on Earth—big, yellow, and warm.

Sun rays filtered through the window, giving Hayley's hair a golden shine, making her look like a queen with a bright crown. She was so beautiful with her delicate features, smooth skin, and pink lips. And when she fixed those sea-green eyes on me, I forgot how to breathe.

My gaze found her ear. She had been so lost deep inside herself, she hadn't even noticed her ears had changed. They were now pointed, not as much as mine, but the typical pointed ear of a half-fae.

She was also half human, and humans were fragile and needed more sustenance and rest than fae. With that in mind, I drove for a couple more hours to let her sleep, then stopped by a quiet diner just outside a small town.

"What is it? What happened?" Hayley sat up and looked around. She narrowed her eyes at the diner in front of us. "Where are we?"

"Honestly, I have no idea," I told her. "But I know you should eat."

"I'm not hungry," she said, her voice low.

I had already gathered she was feisty and stubborn. Things wouldn't be easy with her. "Fine, but I am. You can join me in the diner, or you can wait here."

I exited the car and walked to the diner. Sure enough, Hayley followed me a few heartbeats later. As we stepped through the door, I glamoured our ears, so the humans wouldn't detect anything different.

The diner was small, with only a dozen tables, and only two of them were occupied, plus an elderly man seated at the counter around the kitchen.

I sank into a corner both and picked up the greasy menu from the corner of the table. Her lips turned downward, Hayley sat across from me. I handed her one of the menus.

She pushed it aside. "I'm not hungry."

Holy petals. What would it take for her to give in just this once?

A gray-haired waitress approached us, and I ordered omelet, bacon, French toast, and black coffee for two with my broken English. The old woman smiled and hurried off to work on the order.

Hayley snatched the salt and pepper resting in the center of the table and played with them.

I wanted to make her talk to me, but I didn't know what to ask. "How are you?" didn't seem appropriate right now.

Thankfully, she saved me from that by speaking first. "Where are we going?"

"I was just driving without any direction, just to put some distance between us and your last known location."

Her brows slanted down. "So, what's your plan? Just drive and drive until we reach the ocean on the other side of the country?"

I let out a sigh. "You know my plan. I want you to come with me to the Spring Court, so we can start planning how to take the throne back."

She dropped the salt and pepper and leaned back on the

booth. "Have you considered that I don't want that? I don't want to be queen. I don't want to reignite a freaking war!"

Some eyes turned to us when she raised her voice.

"Right, announce to the world that we're not humans," I said in a low voice.

"I *am* human," she hissed at me.

"Half human," I corrected her.

"I'm purposely forgetting that other part of me. I don't want anything to do with it. And I would like to go back home and return to my life."

"You won't last three hours if you go back. Holy petal, you won't last thirty minutes. They will be waiting for you. The moment they see you coming, they will attack."

Hayley slapped the table but quickly pulled her hand back and glanced out the window. "I didn't sign up for this. I'll just tell them I don't want any throne. They can rest assured I'll forget all about the fae and thrones and whatever else they are worried about. They will leave me alone."

I shook my head. "You're being naive."

"Hey!"

"It's true," I said, fighting to not explode on my queen. In the flower's name, would it always be like this? Arguing and defying the common sense that was right before her eyes? "You saw what they did. They destroyed your house. They killed your mother. They would have killed you just like that —" I snapped my fingers— "if we had given them the chance."

The waitress came back with our food, and I quieted down. Noticing the tension at our table, the waitress just asked if we needed anything else then walked away.

Nose wrinkling, Hayley stared at her plate before pushing

it away. "I need to go to the restroom." She stood. I stood with her. Her eyes rounded at me. "What are you doing?"

I pointed to the small hallway where the sign for the restrooms were located. "I was—"

"No, you weren't," Hayley cut me off. "I can manage to use the restroom by myself. You stay and eat."

She whirled on her heels and went to the restroom.

I exhaled and shoved some of the bacon in my mouth. At least the food in the human world was still as good as I remembered. Next, I ate the omelet, but while I chewed, I kept thinking of Hayley. Every few seconds, I stole a glance at the hallway, waiting to see Hayley walking back to the table. I knew she needed some time alone, but I became anxious if she wasn't where I could see her.

Which was crazy, because I had met her just a few hours ago. And now I was anxious if she stayed away for too long.

I shook my head, trying to relax.

But, after three minutes, my heartbeat sped up. Where the hell was she?

I got up and walked to the restroom door. I knocked on it. "Hayley?" There was no answer. "Hayley?" I called out louder. Still no answer. I pushed the door open and found the restroom empty. What the blossom? I glanced around, my breath becoming shallow. "Hayley!" There was a glass door leading outside just beside the restroom. I looked out, and sure enough, there she was, running away on the side of the road.

Suddenly angry, I took off after her. With my legs much longer than hers and my full-blooded fae powers, I was much faster than her. I reached her in just a few seconds, just as she turned a corner on one of the town's streets.

I grabbed her arm and pushed her against the wall, ready to yell at her.

Then I remembered she was my queen and I shouldn't do that. I swallowed my anger as she pushed hard on my chest. "Let me go!"

"I can't," I said with a long breath. "Even if you don't want to take the throne and be a queen, I can't leave you, because if I do, you're as good as dead."

She punched my chest. "I don't care! I just want this nightmare to end."

I stepped closer to her, and she went completely still, her back straight against the wall.

"My queen," I said, my breath catching. Being this close to her, it was too much. "I'm trying very hard to be respectful and play nice, but when it comes to saving your life, I won't hesitate. You might be mad at me, but I won't care."

She stared at me, her sea-green eyes wide, her breathing coming out in rapid puffs. For a moment, I was lost in her, in her gaze, in the small curve of her high cheekbones, in the roundness of her lips.

She was too blooming beautiful.

I inhaled deeply, taking a little of her lavender scent, and—

The hair at my nape rose on end, and I stiffened. With slow steps, I looked around the corner. Sure enough, Spring Court soldiers entered the diner, looking for us.

"Holy petals," I muttered.

"What is it?" Hayley asked from behind me.

I took her hand in mine again. "Sorry for touching you again, my queen, but we need to be fast."

"What do you—" She yelped when I tugged and ran, pulling her with me to the car. If it were up to me, I would have used the medallion right then, but Hayley would hate me if I did. So we ran toward the car, and I hoped we were fast enough to slip inside and drive away before the Spring soldiers noticed what was going on.

Alert, I sprinted until we were at the back of the car. I grabbed Hayley's shoulders to shove her past the passenger door, but I froze as more Spring soldiers appeared.

I pulled Hayley closer to me and looked around. A dozen Spring soldiers surrounded us, their spears pointed at Hayley. The three others who had gone inside the diner stepped out.

"Well, well, who do we have here?" General Xuan said as he walked among the circle of soldiers. Under my skin, my blood boiled. All I wanted was to seize one of those spears and bury it in his chest. A fake grin spread over Xuan's lips. "General Ashton and Princess Hayley. It's so nice to meet you, Your Highness." He bowed his head at Hayley, though he was clearly mocking her. The grin faded. "Shame I won't get to know you better."

I slipped my hand down Hayley's arms and clutched her hand in mine. "Are you ready?" I whispered to her.

"For what?" she whispered back, her breathing accelerated.

"To go home," I told her. I fished the medallion from the pocket of my pants.

Xuan's dark green eyes rounded at the sight of the medallion in my hand. "Kill them!" he shouted.

"No, wait!" Hayley screamed.

I closed my hand around the medallion, and the world faded away.

THE WORLD WHIRLED AROUND ME. When it finally stopped, my head still spun and my stomach twisted in knots. I pressed a hand to my belly, hoping I didn't throw up.

I took in a lungful of fresh air, and the dizziness slowly went away.

"Are you okay, my queen?"

I glanced to Ashton. Despite the fact that whenever I looked at the chiseled warrior I felt incredibly hot, what I noticed wasn't him.

It was the world around him.

The forest around us seemed to be a live painting of tall trees with bright green leaves and multicolored flowers. A pink butterfly flew past Ashton's head, shining as if there was a neon light in its wings. Two squirrels raced up a tree trunk. I took a step closer, snapping a twig under my shoes. One of them froze and changed from its light brown color to a green one, blending with the tree's leaves.

"Here," Ashton said, touching a patch of purple flowers. They moved with his hand, following his touch. When he retracted his hand, the flowers closed their petals, as if trying to hold him close.

My jaw on the ground, I touched the flowers. They felt velvety and magical, tickling my skin.

"This is amazing," I whispered, enchanted by this marvelous place.

One corner of Ashton's lips turned up as he beckoned me forward. "Come on."

Gawking at everything, I followed as he weaved through the forest, zigzagging past trees, flower bushes, and rocks jutting out of the ground. Soon, we reached a narrow stone path. A moment later, the trees gave way to a clearing and a small chalet. From the dust over the light brown roof and windows and the spiderwebs on the porch, I guessed it had been abandoned for a long time.

"What is this place?" I asked as we reached the porch.

"I used to come here to go hunting with my father."

I frowned. "Where are your parents now?"

"Dead, along with everyone else I cared about." He turned to me and locked his green eyes on mine, and I suddenly felt very small. The man was almost a head taller than me and a lot wider. Not to mention his muscles. Even under his fitted tee, I could see the outline of his many muscles through the fabric.

I swallowed hard. "What is it?"

"Now I care about you," he said. My heart skipped a beat. "As my queen," he added quickly. "Now you're here, and I want to officially pledge my allegiance to you." He knelt in front of me and lowered his head. "All you have to do is accept. Just tell me you'll let me help you get the throne back."

I took a step back. "I don't want to be queen. I just want my life back."

Ashton rose to his full height. "I'm afraid that life is gone, my queen. As I explained many times, if you go back, Vasant will have you killed on the spot."

I shook my head. "I can't believe that." I gestured to the area around us. "I can't believe in any of this. If you ask me, I'm having a very long dream right now. Soon, I'll wake up in my bed and my mother will be making us breakfast before we have to leave to open the flower shop." A lump rose to my throat, and I blinked back sudden tears. In the beginning, I might have thought my mother and Ashton were crazy, but I knew now that wasn't the case, as I knew this wasn't a dream.

"I'm sorry for all that's happened," Ashton whispered. "I'll forever feel shame for not having protected your mother just as fiercely as I was protecting you."

I wiped unshed tears. It hadn't been his fault. She had been the one to throw herself in front of me and take the killing blow instead of me—something I believed any mother would have done for her children. That didn't mean it was easy to accept that she was gone.

And I was all alone in this world.

"Let's say I'm in," I mused, just because I couldn't think of anything else I could do right now. "Let's say I accept this role and I accept your allegiance. Then what?"

"Then I'll teach you to harness your magic while I gather an army that will fight for you," Ashton said, his voice full of hope.

"Fight. That means people will die for me."

"That happens when there's a war."

I let out a long sigh. "I don't want anyone dying for me."

"It won't be just for you," Ashton said. "It'll be for a better future for the Spring Court."

Not being able to handle the fervor in Ashton's eyes, I lowered my gaze. And saw the blood caked over a rip on the sleeve of his shirt. "You're hurt."

He glanced down at his arm. "It's fine."

I reached over and lifted the short sleeve of his shirt. A thin but nasty gash cut across his upper arm. It wasn't bleeding anymore, but it looked angry. "This isn't fine. If we don't clean it right, it'll get infected."

I wrapped my hand around his wrist, opened the wooden door, and entered the chalet. I didn't pay much attention to the place, though I noticed there was a seating area with a leather couch and a big stone fireplace, a dining area with a long wooden table and six chairs, and the kitchen to the right, where I was headed.

"My queen," Ashton called me.

"Hm?" I asked, starting to open the kitchen cabinets, which were mostly empty, looking for a first aid kit.

"If you're looking for medicine and healing ointments, it's in the closet between the bedrooms." He pointed to the small hallway on the other side of the living room.

"Oh." I made my way back, pushed him down on the dusty couch, and went to this closet. It was crammed with towels and bedding and a small wooden box. I opened it and found clean rags and small flasks with dark-colored liquids. I held the box in my hands. "Is this it?" Ashton nodded. I went back to him, but only to put the box in the couch. I opened the curtains of the chalet, letting more light in. Then I sat down on the couch beside him. I laid the box on my lap and picked up the vials. "So, Ashton, which one of these will clean your wound?"

Ashton stared at me, his eyes bright. "Call me Ash," he said in a low voice.

Ash. I kind of liked that. I cleared my throat, focusing back on the task at hand. "All right, Ash, which one?"

Breaking the stare, Ash snatched one of the vials from the box. "This one will clean." Then he grabbed a short tube. "And this one is a paste to help with healing."

I shifted the box to the low table in front of the couch, took a clean rag from the box, and grabbed both medicines from Ash. As I rolled up the short sleeve of his T-shirt, I noticed the many scars across his skin. Some seemed very old and faint, but a few seemed pretty recent. Didn't my mother tell me he had been captured fifteen years ago and recently escaped?

I frowned, wanting to ask him about the scars, but sure this would be an uncomfortable subject. So, as I turned the vial over the rag, letting a few drops fall, and gently brushed the rag over the cut, cleaning the crusted blood, I went for another topic. "I'm guessing this box has been untouched for at least fifteen years, which means all of the contents inside might have expired by now. If you wake up tomorrow and your arm fell off, we'll know."

Again, one corner of Ash's lips tugged up, teasing me and making my heart speed up. By now, I was dying to make him smile for real. I bet his handsome face would brighten even more.

"Fae medicine lasts a long time, way longer than humans'," he explained.

"Good to know." I applied a little more force on the corner of the cut, where the dried blood seemed to have stuck really good, and Ash hissed. I pulled my hands back. "Shit, I'm sorry."

"No, it's fine." His gaze found mine again. So intense, so breathtaking. "What I'm actually struggling with is the fact that my queen is taking care of me. It should be the opposite."

He and this "my queen" thing again. I was getting tired of telling him not to call me that. Trying to keep the mood light, I shrugged. "Well, get used to it. If I ever become queen, I'll be a pretty unruly one."

His brows hiked up. "This means... you're actually considering it? You will stay and fight with me?"

Damn it. That wasn't it, not really. "I didn't say that." I dropped the rag on the table and grabbed the tube. Like a toothpaste, I squeezed the tube and a little dark green paste came out. I gently rubbed that over Ash's cut.

Ash wound both his hands in mine and lowered my arm to his lap. "But you're thinking about it."

Right then, lost in the bright green of his eyes, I would have agreed to anything—especially to getting naked right then and there. But this was much bigger than me. Raising an army? Fighting a war? Being a queen? I wasn't made for that.

I pulled my hand away from him. "Ash—"

The words died on my tongue when I saw a figure standing behind Ash.

ALL OF A SUDDEN, Hayley froze and her eyes, fixed on something right over my shoulder, went wide.

Without thinking, I took my sword from the table and shot up, pointing the blade at whoever was standing there.

But the moment I saw her, my shoulders relaxed and I lowered my sword. "Mahaera."

The goddess smiled. "I see you've succeeded."

I nodded. "Hayley, this is Mahaera, one of the goddesses in Wyth."

Still very pale, Hayley stood up and lowered her head. "Um, hi."

"You don't bow to me, dear. You don't bow to anyone," Mahaera told her. She then turned to me and handed me a big basket she had been holding. "Here. Be a darling and start on supper. I bet Hayley is starving."

I took the basket from the goddess. "Sure," I mumbled, dragging my feet to the kitchen.

"Now, let's talk." Mahaera approached Hayley and sat down

on the couch, right where I had been a moment ago. Mahaera patted the couch, and Hayley sat beside her. "I can sense your apprehension, and I wanted to let you know that's normal."

As I deposited the basket on the counter and started unloading all the goods Mahaera had brought, I paid attention to their conversation. With her sweet grin and soothing voice, Mahaera seemed like one of those healers in the human world who treated the mind. It always baffled me how similar and yet so different the three goddesses were—Mahaera, Mahaeru, and Mahaere. Each of them had a completely different personality. While Mahaeru was serious and business like, Mahaere was feisty and loud. And Mahaera was gentle and kind, just what Hayley needed at the moment.

With a sigh, I washed some of the vegetables Mahaera had brought and put them over a cutting board.

"It's just... everything sounds so crazy," Hayley admitted in a low tone.

"I understand, dear." Mahaera patted her hand. "But it's not crazy. Everything you've been told so far is the truth. If you don't take the throne back, the fake king will destroy the Spring Court, and a bloody war will start against other courts." She paused. "During this war, many courts will perish under Vasant's forces."

"But isn't Vasant the late king's brother? He has as much claim to the throne as I do," Hayley said while I chopped the vegetables.

Mahaera nodded. "That is true, but nobody wants a tyrant on the throne. Vasant doesn't care about the people. All he cares about is power, and he'll only stop once he has control over the entire Wyth. If you rise and prove to the

Spring Court fae that you're better than Vasant, they will support you."

I transferred the chopped vegetables to a pot and filled it with water from the jar Mahaera had brought. I made a mental note to go to the well in the back later and bring more water in. That was if the well still had any water in it.

"Isn't there anyone else who can become queen or king of the Spring Court?" Hayley asked. The tone of her voice and her question cut through me, bringing in a wave of disappointment, but I didn't let it overtake me. Like Mahaera said, Hayley was just apprehensive. She just needed a little more time. "No one from the royal family? How about some other noble?"

"To be honest, yes, you have an aunt and cousins hiding in the Summer Court, but they gave up on their own court a long time ago. They can't do what has to be done to take over the throne. Only you can."

"And what has to be done?" Hayley asked, filling my chest with hope. Now that was a question I liked to hear. I let out a sigh of relief as I lit the cooking fire and placed the pot over it.

"For now, all you have to do is stand up tall and be yourself. The rest will come later." Mahaera reached to the floor and handed a leather bag to Hayley. Where had that bag been? "Here. There are clothes in there, along with some other things you might need." She stood, pulling Hayley with her. "Why don't you go to the bedroom and take a long, relaxing bath. It'll help you process all of this. And once you come out, General Ashton will have supper ready for you."

Hayley stared at the bag in her arms, then at the goddess. I thought she would argue, but to my surprise, she nodded, spun around, and walked into one of the two bedrooms —mine.

When the door closed, Mahaera turned to me. "I've got some things for you too, like clothes, coins, and more." She placed another bag over the couch. "If you go outside, you'll see a horse tied to the porch. He's fine for now, but don't forget to feed him."

I added more saffron to the vegetable soup while it cooked over the fire. "Thank you."

Mahaera shook her head. "Don't thank me just yet. You'll need to be very patient with Hayley. It'll take her a while to accept all the changes in her life and what she has to do. You'll also need to be patient with everything else. It won't be easy to raise an army that can defeat Vasant's forces, and it might take a long time."

"I would like to believe I mastered the art of patience after being tortured for almost fifteen years, but that's not true." I stirred the vegetable soup with a wooden spoon. "I feel like we need to act now or all will be lost."

Mahaera offered me a comforting smile. "Everything is well right now. Just keep moving forward. Small steps." Suddenly, she raised her arm, a folded beige paper in her hand. "Oh, I almost forgot." She handed me the paper. "Queen Natsia had that. Your message was delivered, and that was the response."

Holding my breath, I quickly unfolded the paper and read the message. "They want to meet tomorrow." I looked up at the goddess, glad we were moving forward, just like she said.

"Small steps, remember?" She patted the counter. "All right. I should go now."

"Thank you," I said again. For all the goddesses were doing, I would never be able to thank them enough.

Mahaera frowned. I hadn't had much contact with any of

the goddesses before. The only time I saw them was whenever they came to talk to King Eden, which hadn't been often. In the past, they had rarely addressed me. But I knew them, and I knew each of their personalities.

Frowning wasn't something Mahaera did very often.

"Be careful, General Ashton."

12

I CLOSED the bedroom door behind me and stopped. That had been a goddess. I had just spoken to a goddess, and she held my hand as if she really cared about me.

That was... insane.

I dropped the bag on the bed and took a glance around the bedroom. It was small but quaint, with a big, wooden bed with a tall headboard against one wall, one nightstand beside the bed with a small lantern on it and some sort of lighter on the side, a tall dresser and an armchair on the other side. Like the blanket over the bed, the curtains covering the window were covered in a thin layer of dust. I picked up the bag again. I would have to clean this room before sleeping in here.

Shit, what was I thinking? As if I would stay here.

As if I would fight alongside Ash.

No, I wanted to go back home.

But my mother wasn't there anymore. My best friend had also moved on and was calling me less and less. I had no one. Just the shop. While here, it seemed an entire kingdom depended on me.

It felt like a huge weight pressing down on my shoulders.

I couldn't be responsible for the fate of the Spring Court. It was too much for me.

Tired, I folded the dusty blanket and put it over the armchair. I would wash it somehow tomorrow. Shit, I had to wash everything, even the floors. Didn't fae magic do this? Couldn't I just snap my fingers and have the house cleaned in an instant? Now, that would be a spell I could get behind.

I shook my head. There went my thoughts again.

Shit.

I just wanted to relax.

Following Mahaera's advice, I went into the adjacent bathroom but halted at the doorway. There was a short pillar with what looked like a basin over it, a mirror on the wall behind it, and a big wooden tub in the middle. No faucets, no showers.

Hm, how the hell was I supposed to take a bath?

Without a choice, I exited the bedroom and looked out. Ash wasn't in the living room, and the kitchen seemed quiet. I took three steps forward and halted before the open door to the other bedroom. I knocked on the door, but my hand stilled when I caught sight of Ash standing beside the bed, his back to me, wearing only jeans.

For a moment, I gawked at him, not just because of the many muscles that popped as he moved but also the many scars that marred his skin.

He quickly picked up a shirt, put it on, and turned to me. "How can I help you, my queen?"

I cringed. "First, drop the formalities. I'm not a queen. Right now, I'm your friend." He frowned, probably not convinced. Whatever. "Second, I need help with the bathtub. I don't know how to fill it up."

"Oh, right. I'll help you."

As Ash followed me into the other bedroom and into the bathroom, I asked, "Where's Mahaera?"

"She's gone." He walked around the tub and pointed to a small square on the wall, held by hinges. "See this?" He lifted that thin square up, revealing a pump and the opening of a pipe. He picked up a medium bowl from inside the tub, placed it underneath the pipe, and started pumping the lever. "If you do this, the water from the well will come." It took him a few minutes, but finally the water sputtered and filled the bowl. Then he transferred the water to the tub before doing it all again. "I guess the well still has water," he said.

"Hm, that seems like a lot of work," I said, walking to him. "I can do that."

"No, it's okay. I'll do it for you, my queen."

That term grated at my nerves. I hadn't asked him to do this. I inhaled deeply before actually voicing what was on my mind. "Ash, if I ordered you as your queen to take me back to the human world, would you do it?"

Ash's hand paused and the water cut off. Still kneeling beside the pump, he turned and faced me. "It would go against every one of my instincts, and it would break my soul, but yes, if you ordered me to take you back, I would."

He picked up the half-filled bowl, transferred the water to the tub, placed the bowl on the floor, then went to the other side of the tub. There, he grabbed something like matches and lit a fire on a specific place underneath the tub.

"This will heat up the water?" I asked.

Ash stood. "Yes, my queen. You should wait a few minutes for the water to warm up. Then you can take your bath. When you're ready, come to the dining table for supper."

Without looking at me, Ash marched out of the bathroom. A moment later, I heard the click of the bedroom door closing.

Shit. Just by asking that question, I had already broken his soul, and I felt horrible for it.

I felt horrible for a lot of things at the moment, but most of all, I felt lonely. Abandoned. It hadn't been a day since my mother was gone, and I already missed her desperately.

Tears swelled in my eyes, and this time I didn't hold them back.

I crouched down on the floor and cried.

I LAY down on the floor and stared to the ceiling, the flames from the lantern in the corner creating weird shadows on the walls.

Now that I was here, now that I had stopped for a moment, the horrors of the past decade and a half came rushing into me as if a gate had been opened. I didn't think I could turn off the lantern and sleep. Holy petals, I didn't think I could sleep at all. Each time I closed my eyes, I remembered the pain, the screams, the mind games. And if I happened to sleep, nightmares assaulted my mind.

And now there was Hayley.

She hadn't come out for supper earlier. I thought about knocking on her bedroom door and asking her if she was okay, but after the question she asked me—if I would take her back to Earth if she asked—I thought she was trying to avoid me. Perhaps she was thinking on the subject, or perhaps she had already decided and was concerned about asking me....

Meanwhile, my insides twisted with a concern of my own. I didn't want her to leave. I didn't want her to ask me to take her back. Not just because I felt a pull toward her I couldn't explain, but because I needed her here. She had heard Mahaera. She was the only one who could save the Spring Court from its destruction.

That statement alone probably made her want to run away.

I couldn't blame her for wanting to leave. But I had to do my best to make her want to stay.

But how?

At some point, I must have fallen asleep, because when I turned on my side on the hardwood floor, light from outside filtered through the window, past the half-closed curtains.

After pushing to my feet and stretching, I washed up in the adjacent bathroom and changed into clean clothes— brown trousers and a beige tunic. I threw the jeans and shirt and leather jacket from Earth in the trash.

Then I went to check on Hayley and make us breakfast, but when I opened my bedroom doors, I saw hers was open too. Frowning, I looked inside. She wasn't there. I shuffled my feet into the living room and looked around. She was nowhere I could see.

"Hayley?" I asked as a sliver of panic made its way into my veins. "Hayley!" I called out louder. For leaves' sake, where did she go? Had she left? Run away? But where would she have gone?

My heart beating out of my chest, I raced out of the chalet and looked around.

"Good morning."

Hayley's voice was like a cool balm over a burn wound. I

let out a long breath as I saw her, just outside the porch, her hands tucked in the flowerbed that wrapped around the house.

"Morning," I muttered, approaching her. She was wearing a simple, light green dress that went too well with her sea-green eyes. The faint sunlight shone down on her, and her blonde hair gleamed. My heart squeezed. "I'm guessing Mahaera brought you that dress yesterday?"

She nodded. "Yes. This and a few more, all the same style, which I assume is the Spring Court's style."

For lesser fae, yes. That was fine for now, while Hayley had to blend in with the rest of us. "Why are you out here?"

She shrugged. "I didn't sleep well." She moved her hand, and the flowers moved along with her touch. "I woke up pretty early and decided to check out the area around the house." She smiled when a flower closed its petal around her fingers. My breath caught. Holy petals, could she be any more beautiful? "I think I'm in love with the flowers here."

"They seem to like you too."

She looked at me, still smiling. Then her smile faded and she frowned. "How do you know I would be a good queen?"

"What?" I asked. Where did that come from?

"What if I'm an evil witch and worse than Vasant?"

That was ridiculous. "My queen," I started. She shot me a glare. I didn't care. She was my queen, and I would address her as such. I had to, otherwise I would forget her title and my lowly position in all of this. "You're King Eden's daughter, who was the most generous and kind king the Spring Court had ever had. I believe he passed on those traits to you."

"You don't even know me," she whispered.

Why did that sentence bother me so much? "I don't, but I

have faith you'll be better than Vasant." An idea popped in my mind. "Come on. Let's eat breakfast." After not eating anything last night, she had to be starving. "Then I'll show you something."

"What is it?"

A half smile spread over my lips. "We're going out."

ASH GUIDED the horse through the forest for about an hour. Then we reached a narrow dirt road and followed it for another thirty minutes, until it ended at the gates of a sprawling village, Verdante, as Ash had told me. Here, all the houses looked like the chalet—beige-colored walls, brown roofs, and lots and lots of vines and plants and flowers.

On the way here, Ash had applied a glamour over us both. According to him, he elongated my ears to look like a full-fledged fae and darkened my hair a little bit. As for himself, he grew a short beard and also changed his hair color, but he made his very light, almost white. He warned me that glamours didn't work well for other fae, so I had to be careful. The glamour would disappear if I touched a fae— except for him, since he had been the one to apply it on us.

We rode along the main street cutting through the village, and I drank it all in. Stores lined the street—alchemy and herbs, apparel, furniture, butcher's shop. There were even a few taverns and inns, reminding me of all the fantasy movies I had watched when younger.

When we reached the large square in the middle of the village, Ash jumped off the horse and offered me his hand. I hesitated but took it, letting him help me get off the horse. "Wait here," he said, before guiding the horse to a street corner, where other horses were tethered.

But I couldn't stop gawking at the village's square. Kids played with a small ball, but instead of kicking it or throwing it, they either moved the earth or the plants around them to keep the ball rolling. Women danced with little girls, moving their arms and hips in a way that reminded me of flamenco. Ash explained they were from a dance school and were doing a demonstration. Further in the square, there was an extensive garden, where fae displayed their incredible powers—more plant and earth playing.

Carts that reminded me of food trucks were stationed around the square, selling food. Ash bought a honey cake for us.

"This is typical fae food, common and favored in all of Wyth," he said before taking a big bite out of his cake.

I sniffed it first. Of course, it smelled of sweet, sweet honey. But when I bit into it, I had to swallow a moan. Holy shit, the cake was delicious.

I heard a sniff to my left. When I looked down, I saw a kid staring at the honey cake cart with huge eyes. The little girl was dirty and shoeless. I frowned. So far, I hadn't seen anyone looking like her here.

"Are you hungry?" Ash asked her. The little girl nodded. Without any hesitation, Ash bought an extra honey cake and handed it to her. The girl showed him a huge smile before thanking him and dashing away, her mouth full of the food.

Twice more, Ash showed me his big heart. Once when the ball from the kids' game rolled too far away from them but right by our side. To keep the game going, Ash summoned vines and swung the ball to the kids, who cheered at him. Then an elderly woman carting a big load of paintings struggled to cross the street into the square. Again, Ash didn't hesitate. He just sprang into action and helped the woman with her load.

The way he gave to his people and helped them, as if that was tied to his blood, as if he couldn't stop himself from helping everyone... it was touching. It made me feel proud to know him, to have him by my side.

On a corner, an instrument shop set up a demonstration. Fae came in and played instruments—some I had never seen before—while others danced to the music. It was like line dancing. Two started dancing together and the others followed. I felt entranced by their moves, wishing I could dance like that. I only noticed I was trying to imitate them when Ash grabbed my hand in his and pulled me amid the other dancing fae.

"What are you doing?" I whispered.

"Dancing with you," he said simply. I was still for a moment while Ash stepped around me, following the beat of the song. "Just mirror my movements."

As if that was easy. Not when this gorgeous man danced around me, flexing his arms, bulging the muscles of his shoulders, swaying his hips side to side, his green eyes fixed on mine. Holy shit, he was just... perfect. Ash was kind, brave, and hot. He made my heart beat faster just by standing in front of me.

My throat dry, I forced myself to move with him. After all, it wasn't every day that I had a godlike man wanting to touch me like that. He wound his arm around my waist and spun me around and under his arm; then he caught me again and threw me back, dipping my torso. His eyes were still on mine, but his head was aligned with my chest. If he leaned one inch closer, he could lick my breasts.

Heat spread through my body.

I knew there were many couples dancing exactly like us, but I couldn't help the feelings coursing through me; the want, the desire.

As if I had been hit in the head, I realized that despite everything, I wanted Ash. Even if it was for one night, I wanted him to explore every inch of my body, to ravage me, to take me to heights I had never been before.

Self-conscious of my thoughts, I stopped dancing and stepped back.

"Everything all right?" Ash asked, his brows slanted down.

"Hm, yeah, I just... I need some water." Wasn't that the truth? I needed water to quench this heat burning inside me.

Ash nodded and beckoned me to follow him. We walked away from the green and into a smaller street leading away from the village's center. Stopping at a corner, Ash opened the door to a shop.

"What is this place?" I asked, suddenly worried.

"It's a famous teahouse in the village," he said, gesturing for me to enter. I went in with Ash and took a seat at a table just beside the large window on the second floor overlooking the street. A waitress came by, and he ordered a tea for me.

"Thank you," I said to the waitress when she returned with my tea and placed it in front of me.

Once she was gone, Ash said, "Drink this and only this."

"Why? What if I want to order something else?"

He shook his head. "Don't. Most drinks and food you'll find here will be poison for a human."

"As far as I know, I'm not just a human."

"Correct, but we don't know how it would affect a half-fae. Until then, don't drink or eat anything." He stood up.

I frowned. "Where are you going?"

"I have something to do," he said, his voice tight. Was he mad at me because I stopped dancing with him? Shit, I hoped not. "Remember, don't talk to anyone, don't touch anyone. Wait for me here. I'll be back soon."

Before I could protest or ask more questions, Ash walked out of the teahouse, leaving me alone in a strange world.

I DIDN'T LIKE LEAVING Hayley alone at the teahouse, but it was better than bringing her with me. I didn't know how this would go, and I had to make sure she remained safe.

After exiting the teahouse, I went deeper into Verdante to a poorer part of the village. The scenery changed. From well-kept shops and streets and smiling fae to streets full of holes, dirt, and broken building facades and lesser fae starving and sick.

The scene twisted my stomach. It hadn't been this bad when King Eden was on the throne. I remembered it getting worse during the war; after all, our attention was taken while we tried to keep the entire court from being killed, but now it felt like a nightmare had taken over.

How could Vasant sleep at night knowing his subjects lived like this?

Following the note Mahaera had given me, I went into an alley and opened the black door at the back. From there, I climbed down the narrow steps until they ended into what looked like a long, wide underground tunnel. Stands ran alongside the tunnel walls, selling everything—healing herbs, medicine, free passage to Earth or other realms, drugs, slaves, and more.

If this place existed while Eden was the king, I hadn't known, but I wanted to pretend it didn't. I wanted to believe this place came to be after Vasant took over and made their lives so miserable the fae had no choice but to sell anything in order to survive.

I followed along the tunnel until I found the large red tent that sold witch drinks. I ducked my head as I stepped in and immediately found them.

Ilan, Leif, and Gul sat on stools in the corner of the tent, a small, bent metal table in front of them with many colored drinks on top.

When they saw me, their eyes went wide.

"I can't believe it," Ilan said, his voice thick.

I took a seat beside them. "You better believe it."

Gul's lower lip trembled. "They told us you died on that terrible day."

My brows slammed down. Really? Had no one known I was being tortured for this long?

Leif slapped a big hand on my shoulder. "I'm just glad you're back."

I looked at each one of them. Like me, Ilan had been a general under King Eden's command. He had been loyal and hardworking and one of the best warriors I had ever met. Leif and Gul had been two of my best soldiers. When I was captured, I thought they had been too. I hadn't heard anything from them or about them in almost fifteen years, so I just assumed the worst.

"I'm glad you're all here," I said. "What have you three been doing all this time?"

Ilan told me he had become a simple merchant, selling leather he skinned from his hunts, while Leif and Gul had become low-ranked soldiers in Vasant's army.

"We didn't have a choice," Leif said. "We tried resisting it, but they kept torturing us."

"General Xuan threatened my mate," Gul said, his tone gloom. Only about 80 percent of the fae found their mates, and once they did, that was it. They never bonded or loved again. Though I hadn't found a mate for myself yet, I understood how it worked, and I understood why Gul had given in. "I couldn't hate the fake king more, but I had no choice."

"I haven't heard many complaints lately, but I remember right after King Eden was killed and many soldiers like us were forced into their service, that the concerns and discontent were voiced loudly," Leif said.

"That's good to know, because I have a request for the three of you," I started, suddenly apprehensive. This was the second big step toward the future. I didn't want to mess it up. "If I assembled an army to fight Vasant, would you join me?"

The three of them gawked at me as if I were speaking gibberish.

"What do you mean?" Ilan asked.

"Ash, I hate Vasant and I would love to bury my sword in his chest, but...." Leif sucked in a harp breath. "Look at all he did. He was able to keep up a war for twenty years; he killed King Eden and his family and obliterated our army. We can't win against him."

"Especially with Sanna by his side," Gul added.

In the flower's name, I had forgotten about the damn witch. She had been beside Vasant since before the war started. In fact, King Eden had told me several times that he thought it was Sanna who had instigated Vasant's hatred for his brother and helped him attack first.

This conversation wasn't going as I expected. "What if I had a weapon that could destabilize them?"

Ilan frowned. "What do you mean?"

I didn't want to tell them about Hayley just yet. I had to keep her existence and whereabouts a secret for as long as I could. "I can't say anything yet. Just... trust me like you used to do fifteen years ago." The three of them exchanged a glance. I understood their hesitation, I really did, but I didn't have time for this. "Come on, comrades. Talk to your fellow soldiers, the ones you said voiced complaints in the beginning. Get them together and let's fight. Let's take our court back."

Leif puffed out his chest. "I'm in!"

Gul groaned. "All right. So am I."

We all looked at Ilan.

Ilan shuddered. "Can I think about it?"

"We don't have time for that," I insisted.

Ilan sighed. "Okay then. I'm in."

"Great!" I almost shouted, feeling more cheerful than I had in a long, long time. I had the queen, and I was starting to build an army. We were still far from where I wanted to be, but we were moving forward. "Talk to the other soldiers who served King Eden. I'll send a message when we need to meet again."

After saying our goodbyes, I walked away and out of the tunnel.

Even though I had to cross through that dark and crude part of town, my steps were lighter than before. It was starting. We were starting. Soon, the Spring Court would be free from Vasant's clutches.

I headed to the teahouse, eager to get to Hayley.

I rounded a corner and halted when I saw soldiers sweeping the street a couple of blocks ahead. They marched into shops and yelled at the fae. They grabbed a young female fae and yanked her forward.

Young female fae with long blonde hair who seemed to be around one hundred and sixty-seventy years old—twenty-one years old for a human.

The blood drained from my veins.

They were looking for Hayley.

NOT A MINUTE after Ash walked away, I became bored. There was nothing to do here, other than just stay seated, look through the window, and do some people watching.

Or fae watching. I was still getting used to seeing so many people with pointed ears and similar physical traits—white-blond to dark-blond hair, green or blue eyes, and fair skin. When I asked about it while Ash and I were at the square, he explained those were the Spring Court traits. That other courts would look different.

I then gestured to a woman with red hair who was dancing with some kids. "She's either from the Autumn Court and decided to live here or she's half-Spring and half-Autumn," Ash explained.

There were only a handful of fae inside the teashop, but from what I could see, all of them had blond hair, though some had short, some had long, or straight or curled. Even with the same colors, each fae was still different.

I took the last sip from the tea Ash had ordered for me. I placed the empty cup on the wooden table, wondering how much longer it would take him to do whatever it was he was doing. I was getting hungry here!

With a sigh, I leaned back on my chair and glanced around just as an elderly female fae entered the teashop carrying a basket with small vials. She went around the tables, talking to the customers and trying to sell her product.

Then she stopped by my table. "Would you be interested in buying a perfume?" the fae asked, her voice frail, but with a sweet smile.

"Hm, no, thank you."

"Are you sure?" The fae glanced around then leaned closer. "I made these with the flowers from King Eden's secret garden." My eyes widened. "Shh." She pressed a finger over her lips. "Haven't you heard about his secret garden? Oh, it wasn't in the palace, you see, because the queen couldn't have known about it. The secret garden was hidden because it was dedicated to the woman he really loved. Some say she was human." She winked. "The garden was forgotten after the royal family was assassinated, but I found it, and now I take care of it."

My hands shook with this revelation. Was this old fae saying nonsense, or could I believe her? "Where is this garden?"

She offered me a soft smile. "If I tell you, then I'll go out of business, won't I? Moreover, the fake king might hear about it and destroy the secret garden, and this is the last piece we have of King Eden." She sighed. "To be honest, I would rather he was still alive and tending to his garden himself. Then we wouldn't be in this terrible situation."

I frowned. "What terrible situation?"

"Oh, haven't you heard? Don't let the events in town trick you," the old fae said. "This is one of the last villages that wasn't destroyed by the fake king. Yet. Wait and see. He'll run us down, and soon we'll all be homeless and starving." She tsked. "Enough of this sad conversation." She lifted the basket an inch. "Last chance. Will you buy one of the secret garden's perfume or not?"

I stared at the vials in the basket. Was she telling the truth? Did this place exist? Had King Eden created it for my mother? I had no ties to him other than having inherited his blood, but for some reason, I wanted more. I wanted the perfumes; I wanted to find the secret garden.

I reached over the basket, intent on picking a vial with a pretty swirl of pink and green liquids, but the old fae stiffened. "Oh no," she muttered, her eyes on the window beside my table. "Here comes trouble."

I followed her gaze. At the end of the streets, soldiers entered a store. A moment later, they came out, carrying a young fae with long, blonde hair. They threw her in the middle of the street and pointed their spears at her.

I gasped. "What's going on?" I asked, but when I glanced back, the old fae was hurrying out of the tavern.

Shocked, I returned my gaze to the commotion on the street. Another group of soldiers exited another shop, carrying a girl who looked like the one on the ground.

A girl who looked like me.

My stomach dropped. They were looking for me.

And they were coming this way.

I knew I was glamoured, but if I came face-to-face with the soldiers, would I be able to suppress my panic? I doubted it. So, even though Ash told me not to move, I shot up and quickly exited the teashop. I headed the opposite way the soldiers were coming and turned on the first street ahead. Even though I was worried about how I would find Ash again, I kept going, I kept moving. I was too afraid to stop and consider what would happen to me if they found me.

But there wasn't much I could do about the panic starting to rise from my chest. My hands shook and my breath grew shallow as I weaved through the streets, trying to put some distance between the soldiers and me.

Then someone barreled into me and pushed me back.

I screamed.

I PRESSED my hand over Hayley's mouth and pushed her further into the narrow alley. She fought against me, but I was too strong for her. I pressed her against a wall just behind an archway. "Shhhh," I told her. "It's me."

Finally seeing me through her despair, Hayley's eyes widened and her body relaxed a little bit. I dropped my hand but didn't let her go.

"Ash," she whispered.

That word, that tone, it hit me directly in my gut. Holy petals, how scared I had been when I realized what was going on. And when I couldn't find her at the teashop? Even worse.

Pure relief coursed through me once I found her.

"They are close," I told her in a low voice. "Just stay still."

I stepped closer to her, pressing my body against her, hiding us from view. Her scent filled my nostrils, and the pull, that same pull I had felt before, tugged hard and deep inside my chest, growing tenfold. It felt like a tangible rope that tied me to her, unbreakable and powerful.

The mating bond.

I stilled, even though I couldn't ignore the way her soft curves molded around my body. She must have felt something too, because her breathing changed and her heart sped up, but it wasn't in fear. She leaned into me, brushing her breasts against my chest.

I gritted my teeth, swallowing a growl.

Hayley was mated to me. My queen was truly mine.

And I wanted her.

I wanted to kiss her, right here, right now.

I wanted to take her.

The soldiers marched on, but I still couldn't move. I still couldn't bring myself to step away from her. I didn't want to. Not now, not ever. Hayley had been made for me.

And yet, this wasn't right. It couldn't be right.

I forced myself to retreat. "They're gone."

Without looking at her, I took her hand in mine and guided her back to where our horse was.

THE RIDE back to the chalet was quiet and tense. With Hayley pressed behind me and her delicate hands around my waist, I couldn't focus. I could barely take us back to the chalet because I kept getting lost with my mind solely on her—on her body, on her hands, on her scent, that had suddenly become so strong and alluring, it was driving me crazy.

When we arrived, I told her to go inside and rest. "I'll take care of the horse first."

She frowned. "Okay."

I knew she noticed something had happened, that something had changed, but I wouldn't crack. Not yet.

Needing some distance from her, I walked into the forest.

I inhaled deeply, welcoming the earth and leaves scents, as if they could erase Hayley from my mind.

A good way from the chalet, I started pacing.

How come I was Hayley's mate? I was of low birth, a lesser fae with no merit, other than my skill in killing others. Hayley was a queen, the heir to our kingdom. She deserved better than a lowly warrior.

My feelings were in turmoil inside me. I wanted to race back and claim her as my own, but my warrior's honor didn't let me.

How in blossom was I going to stand beside her and help her take her court back with my emotions frazzled like this?

"I see the bond snapped," Mahaere said, appearing before me. The fun and eloquent sister. She had her red hair in a complicated braid atop her head, and she wore red trousers and a leather vest with an empty quiver on her back.

I did my best not to yell at the goddess. "Is this a sick joke? Why send me to retrieve her, knowing she's my mate?"

Mahaere smiled. "It's not a joke. It's a happy coincidence. One you must keep hidden from Hayley for a while."

I frowned. Not that I planned on telling her, but I needed to know. "Why?"

"This entire world is still foreign to her," Mahaere said, her voice too happy for this conversation. "She's already feeling confused and lost. If you tell her about fated mates now, and that you're hers, you'll only scare her more. She'll feel pressured, more than she already does. It won't go well."

"You're saying I can't tell her."

Mahaere nodded. "Not yet. Promise me you won't tell her, that you won't act on it."

I let out a long sigh. "I promise."

"Good." She lost her smile. "Now you should go back, before she realizes something is wrong."

Wrong. Was the goddess saying our mating bond was wrong?

But before I could ask her about it, Mahaere disappeared.

I inhaled deeply and started back toward the chalet. As I said I would do, I fed the horse and tended him for a few minutes. But I dropped everything when I saw Hayley walking by the window.

My heart squeezed.

For leaves' sake, I had always found her beautiful. But now? Now she was painfully stunning. I watched her for a minute.

Then another figure appeared in the back of the living room. Hayley wasn't alone.

I pulled out my sword and raced into the chalet.

Ash had been acting strange since we were hiding earlier in the village. At that moment, when he had his rock-hard body pressed against me, I thought I had won. That was the sign I needed to show him I wanted him too. Heat coursed through me, and I couldn't stop myself even if I wanted to.

Right when I reached for him, he pulled back.

After that, he barely looked in my direction. Not while we were getting the horse, or riding back to the chalet, or when we arrived and he sent me inside.

I felt like standing my ground and arguing with him, but about what? That he had been quiet? That I wanted to jump on him and he had suddenly closed himself off? I wouldn't be the first one to confess, much less beg.

So I went inside the chalet. From the corner of the window, I watched as Ash stomped into the forest and disappeared among the trees. What the hell was that?

Tired but starving, I went to the kitchen and started on our dinner. There wasn't much I could do with the ingredients we had, and without human technology it would take forever, but I soon found I could make some chicken rice bake, and that would be enough.

I had just finished and had left the pot over the fire, praying it was enough to cook everything through, when she appeared.

Mahaera smiled at me. "That looks good."

"Hm." I glanced side to side. Should I say hi? Should I bow to a goddess? She had told me not to bow to her before, but that felt so wrong.

"Relax, Hayley, I won't bite."

I leaned on the kitchen counter. "Why do I feel like you came to tell me something bad?"

The goddess let out a small chuckle. "No, nothing bad. At least not for now. I came here to talk to you about Wyth and fae. I bet you're very confused about everything, and I bet General Ashton hasn't really sat down with you and answered your questions." She moved her hand, the long sleeve of her white gown covering the table in the middle of the kitchen. When she pulled her hand away, there were two glasses on the table. She took them both and offered one to me. "Ask me anything."

I grabbed the glass from her, admiring its uniqueness. Thin metal vines painted green wrapped around the stem. Each little thing in this place seemed tailored accordingly to the Spring Court.

I shrugged. "I don't even know what to ask." But then I remembered something. "Today, while I was away with Ash, an old female fae talked to me. She said she knew where King Eden's secret garden was. I asked her to show me, but she said she couldn't. At first, I believed her, but now I'm skeptical. She could be lying."

Mahaera shook her head. "She wasn't. The secret garden exists, though it isn't the place she goes for her flowers."

"She said King Eden had the secret garden done for a lover. A human lover."

"Yes, for your mother. Though they weren't mates, King Eden really loved your mother, in a way he never loved Queen Elowen." She showed me a soft smile. "And he loved you too. That's why he sent you two back to Earth, to keep you both safe, since he couldn't."

From there, Mahaera launched into a long speech about the Spring Court and the entire Wyth. I learned many things about the sight, the speech, about changelings (the exchange with human children, which shouldn't happen anymore), fae food (some of it could make me drunk and some could kill me), and even about iron (it was like poison to the fae). At some point, Mahaera and I moved to the couch while we kept talking.

Another thing I learned was that Wyth was a continent in the fae realm with eight different courts—Spring, Summer, Fall, Winter, Dawn, Day, Dusk, and Night. Each court had different traits, landscapes, traditional cuisine, rules, and magic. In the center of Wyth was a place called Niwtrall, which was inaccessible but made of pure magic. Mahaera told me that Niwtrall and the land of the Wyth continent were alive in some way, and they had a will of their own.

She also told me about the Tywyll Forest to the south of the Winter and Day Courts, a place full of monsters, and an unnamed and inhabited island to the north.

When I asked her about her and her sisters and other gods, Mahaera dismissed my question and went on to tell me about Ashton.

"Ashton came from a lesser fae family," Mahaera said.

"His mother was from the Autumn Court, and his father, Talasi, became a soldier while still young. Talasi rose in ranks fast, becoming one of the king's most trusted generals in record time. Proud of his father, Ashton followed in his footsteps. He was a decorated soldier on his own, but Ashton became a general only after his father died during the war. Then he became the king's most trusted general."

"That's why he feels so guilty about King Eden's death," I muttered, already feeling a little dizzy from the wine. Every time I emptied my glass, more wine magically appeared in it.

Mahaera nodded. "Not only that, he was captured and tortured for almost fifteen years. I know he wished they would have just killed him and ended his suffering, but they kept him there, most days at the brink of death, but they always stopped so he could recover and start all over."

"I didn't know," I whispered, upset with myself. I had known about the torture, yes, but I hadn't really thought about it, considered what it had meant.

My stomach tightened, and I put the glass on the low table before the couch. Poor Ash. I couldn't imagine being tortured for fifteen years. How twisted his thoughts probably were when he was alone, how terrible his nightmares when he was sleeping. I suddenly wished he was here so I could give him a big hug and tell him everything would be okay.

"All right, I think you now know a lot about fae and Wyth," Mahaera said, not sounding a little bit drunk, though I was sure she had consumed more than me. Was that a divine trick? "So we'll start on our next topic."

"Which is?" I asked, curious.

"Your magic," Mahaera said. "General Ashton told me you used your magic once before, even though you had no idea what you were doing." I glanced down at my hands, remembering that odd feeling that had filled my veins. I hadn't tried doing that again. "I would like to teach you how to control your magic, how to use it."

I frowned. "Hm. Is that really necessary?"

"If you join the war with Ashton, yes, it is." Mahaera twirled her hand and a yellow flower appeared atop her open palm. "Ashton will be busy putting an army together. Meanwhile, I can come and teach you about magic."

Magic was cool, at least in theory, but I still didn't know about any of this. Being a queen, engaging in a war.... It all sounded too farfetched for my taste. And now Vasant's soldiers were combing through villages to find me.

I liked all of this less and less.

But I did like the way Ash looked at me when he talked about the future, about how we would regain the Spring Court, help the people, and just save everyone. I felt proud of myself seeing so much hope in his eyes. I wanted to make him proud.

I wanted to do so many things with him.

I placed my hand over my heart as it sped up. Something about Ash called to me. I felt a crazy pull toward him that I couldn't explain. It made me all hot and bothered.

The scent from the rice and chicken bake tickled my nose, and I shot up, glad to have some excuse not to answer Mahaera's offer. "I need to check on dinner." I marched to the kitchen, almost tripping on my own feet. Who told me to drink that much while seated and not eating anything? "It's probably ready."

I turned to the pot on the fire, but I felt Mahaera's shadow approaching me. "I know you're scared. Of Vasant, of the soldiers, of the war, of being queen." She paused. "Of Ashton."

I whipped around, facing the goddess again. "I am not!" I cleared my throat. "Scared of Ash, I mean. He's—"

The chalet's door burst open, startling me.

Ash marched in, his sword raised at Mahaera.

MY STEPS FALTERED, and I quickly lowered my sword when I saw the one with Hayley was Mahaera. "What the—" I pressed my lips tight, a little lost here. Mahaere had just come to see me, and now Mahaera was here.

Were the goddesses playing tricks on us?

I bowed my head. "I apologize, Mahaera. When I saw movement inside, I thought it could be soldiers."

"I understand," Mahaera said, sporting a smile. She gestured to the kitchen. "I think supper is ready."

I glanced at Hayley, and my heart contracted. Was there a time when I would look at her and not feel like my heart was ripping, as if I couldn't breathe if I stayed more than two feet from her, as if I could live on without touching her?

Hayley took the lid off a heavy pot, and a savory scent reached my nose. Whatever it was, it smelled delicious. This time, Hayley was the one to avoid my gaze. She went on about the kitchen, grabbing plates and utensils and setting up the table.

I rushed to her. "Let me help." I took the glasses from the

cabinets and filled them with water.

"Hayley," Mahaera called her. Hayley stiffened before looking at the goddess. "What's your answer?"

I frowned. "What's going on?"

Hayley's sea-green eyes shifted to me for a second. Then she nodded. "All right. I'll train with you."

"Train? Train what?" I asked, feeling anxious about this.

"Hayley agreed to train her magic with me," Mahaera said, sounding pleased.

"She did?" I asked, not believing my ears. "Does this mean you're staying?"

Hayley lowered her gaze. "I don't know."

"It doesn't matter," Mahaera said. "At least she's working on something while she decides. We'll start tomorrow." Mahaera turned, and for a moment I believed she would actually go out using the door. I should have known better. "Oh, before I forget." She faced us again. "The floral nymphs are holding a ceremony at the Greenarch Hill later tonight. I told them you two were going, so they're preparing a blessing for Hayley."

Holy petals. I didn't like how giddy nymphs were and how intense these ceremonies could get, but if Mahaera had arranged a blessing, we had to go. I let out a sigh. "We'll be there."

Hayley stared at me, seemingly lost on what we were talking about. When I looked back at Mahaera, she was gone.

Offering me a plate, Hayley asked, "What was that about?"

I took the plate from her. "Just... let's eat and get ready. The Greenarch Hill isn't around here." I served myself of the food she had made: rice and chicken in a pot together. It looked strange, but it smelled good. So I shoved a forkful in my mouth. Holy petals, this was delicious. Good thing too, because then I kept on eating, and with my mouth full, I couldn't explain anything to Hayley.

The less I talked to her, the better, because truth be told, I wasn't sure how long I was going to be able to keep my promise to Mahaere and stay away from Hayley.

———

IN SILENCE, I helped Hayley clean up the kitchen then went to my bedroom to wash up and change. The visit to the village and all that despair I felt when I couldn't find Hayley made me feel dirty.

I changed into brown trousers and a dark green shirt and made sure my hair was combed back and neat. This outing wasn't much, but it was still an important ceremony, and I felt like I had to dress up.

When I stepped out of my bedroom, Hayley was exiting hers, and my breath caught. She looked beautiful in a light green dress with golden embroidery. She had pulled half of her hair back and tied it in a braid, revealing her long, smooth neck.

My lips itched, wanting to taste her skin.

"Anything wrong?" Hayley asked, rubbing her neck.

I shook my head, clearing my mind and sending the heat in my core away. "No. Are you ready?"

She nodded.

We took the horse, and I guided him through the forest, going north toward the Greenarch Hill. At this time of the night, pink fireflies hovered in the air, and some leaves shone bright whenever the horse's legs touched them, lighting the way.

With her chest pressed to my back and her hands on my waist, Hayley seemed enchanted by the world around her. My heart squeezed when I glanced over my shoulder and saw the wonder in her eyes.

In the flower's name, this wasn't easy. How was I supposed to stay still when she was so beautiful, so innocent, and looked so amused by her own court? I was starting to think that staying by her side might not be the best idea. I probably should send her away with Mahaera while I organized all the rest. Besides being safer with the goddesses, I would focus on what I should: finding an army.

Otherwise... otherwise, I wasn't sure what would happen.

About ten minutes into the ride, Hayley spoke. "Will you explain to me what's going on and where we are going?"

Holy petals, I had forgotten I hadn't told her about it yet. "Nymphs are powerful beings. They possess a unique kind of magic that ties them to the land. They can bless fae with their powers, which makes the blessed one very lucky. Mahaera set it up so they will bless you tonight during one of their ceremonies."

"Oh" was all Hayley said.

Though the horse Mahaera had given us was fast and strong, it took us over two hours to arrive at the Greenarch Hill.

"We're here," I told Hayley just before we stepped through the last line of trees.

Right in front of us was a low hill, alight with the green-hued moonshine. Atop the hill were long wooden pillars twisted like tree trunks, forming a wide arc on the ground. And among them were the floral nymphs.

"Wow," Hayley whispered, watching them from over my shoulder.

I could understand her admiration or amusement when looking at the nymphs. With their green hair, fair skin with a faint green hue, bright green eyes, and skimpy green dresses that barely covered their long limbs, they were creatures Hayley had never encountered before.

Once they saw us approaching, the nymphs rushed to us. They grabbed us by our legs and arms, practically pulling us down from the horse.

"Hey, slow down," I told them. I never liked how handsy they were, but now it bothered me even more, probably because I didn't like Hayley seeing other women touching me —not that she seemed to care about it.

She smiled at the nymphs while they ran their hands over her shoulders, smelled her hair, poked her cheeks. Hadn't the nymphs seen a half human before? Despite her ears, which were just slightly less pointed than ours, Hayley could pass for a normal fae.

The nymphs giggled as they guided us to the top of the hill, among the pillar arch, where they pampered us up. On me, they put a yellow and orange flower necklace and mussed my hair, so it was all messed up around my head. On Hayley, they placed a pink flower crown atop her head and yellow flower bracelets on her wrists. My heart skipped a beat. How could she look more beautiful with each passing minute? She was just stunning.

"Just stay here," a nymph with short, spiky hair told me, pushing me back a little. As far as I knew, nymphs were mystical beings of few words. I didn't think I had ever heard one speaking before.

Then the spiky-haired nymph took Hayley's hand and brought her right to the center of the pillars. All two dozen of the nymphs knelt around Hayley in a circle. They lifted their hands up to the sky, said something that sounded foreign to me, and then lowered their heads to the ground. They repeated the same action five times, while Hayley stood among them, seeming a little lost.

Seeming like a real queen.

After the bows, the nymphs joined hands and hummed.

Hayley shivered, as if she had felt something.

Then the nymphs clapped and rose to their feet. They embraced Hayley, kissed her hand, and touched her hair.

"You're blessed now," the spiky-haired nymph said. "Your path won't be easy, but you must not give up."

Hayley's eyes found mine. I held her gaze, wondering, wishing she wouldn't give up. That she wouldn't ask me to take her back to Earth. That she would become the queen the Spring Court deserved. That someday when all of this was over, I would be able to confess my feelings to her. Tell her that she was my mate.

Shaking my head, I averted my eyes. I couldn't think about that now. Being her mate wasn't important at this moment. First, we'd deal with Vasant and take back the court. Then we'd worry about the rest.

A couple of nymphs started playing instruments, and a melodious and happy song filled the air. Food and drinks were passed around. The party had started.

"No, no," Hayley said when a nymph gave her a glass full of wine. "I already drank too much tonight."

"It's okay," the nymph said. "This wine is weaker than most."

Hayley hesitated but took the glass.

Intent on not falling into her web, I turned around, just as a nymph brought me a glass of wine. First, I refused, because a warrior shouldn't drink when on duty, and I was always on duty now. But when I glanced over my shoulder and saw Hayley dancing with the nymphs, moving her arms and hips just as sensually as the magical creatures, throwing her head back and exposing that neck and collarbone, twirling until her skirt hiked up, showing most of her legs... I snagged the next glass of wine that appeared in front of me and downed half of it in one big gulp.

For leaves' sake, this was going to be a long night.

The spiky-haired nymph wound her arm around my waist and pushed me toward the group dancing.

"No, I'm good," I told her, gently removing her arm from around me.

"Will you let your mate dance alone?" she asked with a knowing smile.

My eyes widened. "How...?"

She shrugged. "We just know things."

I drank the rest of the wine. "It doesn't matter. I shouldn't act on it."

"The queen won't know that," the nymph said. "She'll just think you're dancing with her. Nothing less, nothing more."

Despite my strong will, I stared at Hayley again. A nymph spun her around, and she let out a loud laugh. The pull that drew me to her tugged hard at my chest. Holy petals, when she looked this carefree and happy, how could I resist her?

"I can't," I mumbled, knowing I was losing the battle. I tried thinking of what Mahaere told me, that I shouldn't let Hayley know about being my mate, not yet, but I could dance with her, right? I had danced with her before and nothing came of that. I was sure I could do it again.

The spiky-haired nymph gave me a little push.

It was all I needed.

A little dizzy from the wine—I hadn't drunk any alcohol

in over fifteen years—I walked to the dancing group. The nymphs, probably as aware that Hayley was my mate as the spikey-haired one, opened up and let me pass. Once I was behind Hayley, I halted.

With a smile, Hayley spun around. Her eyes met mine, and she stopped, her smile widening. For leaves' sake....

Without hesitation, she grabbed my arms and pulled me closer. "I thought you weren't going to join us," she said, her words slightly slurred. She was as dizzy as I was.

"I didn't think I would either," I confessed.

She tilted her head. "What changed your mind?"

You. Right now, you're my strength and my weakness, and I would do anything for you, even dance among floral nymphs. I shrugged. "Just trying to relax a little before we start a war." Which wasn't a lie.

Her smile faded a little. "Can we not talk about the throne, being a queen, and wars tonight?" She put my hands on her waist and stepped into my personal space, winding her arms around my neck. "Let's just have a good time."

She began leading, swaying us side to side. I was too stunned with her closeness, with her sweet scent, with her perfection to do anything other than just gawk at her and move with her cues.

In the flower's name, this was too much and not enough. A growing need to touch her, to pull her to me, to claim her hit me hard, making me feel hot on the inside. My cock hardened, and I spread my legs a little wider, trying to accommodate it.

Suddenly, popping sounds rose louder than the music, grinding at my ears, reminding me of a heavy hammer falling over nails buried in my arms and legs.

In an instant, I had my sword in my hand and Hayley

behind me. My breathing accelerated, I looked around, but all I saw was the nymphs stepping away from us—from me.

The music stopped playing as the spikey-haired nymph approached us. "What is it?" she asked, wary.

"The hammering sound," I said, my voice rough. "I heard something."

"That?" She pointed to a nymph with a metal drum. The nymph bumped the sticks on the drum, and the sound echoed through the night, sending an icy shiver down my back.

I gritted my teeth. "Yes."

"It's just the drum, Ash," Hayley said from behind me. She rested her hands on my shoulders and got closer to me. "They won't play it anymore, right?" She glanced at the spikey-haired nymph from around my arm, her hand snaking down to my arm. She gently pushed my arm down, until my sword was pointing to the ground.

The nymph nodded. "Sure."

My heart thumped fast in my chest, and my hands shook. The music returned, but slower this time and without the drums, but the tension didn't want to leave my body. The memories of those painful days didn't want to leave my mind.

"See? No more drums." Hayley stepped in front of me, her hands coming up and cupping my face. My eyes darted side to side, searching for danger. "Ash, look at me." I forced my gaze to meet Hayley. She had a small smile on her lips. She guided my hand, sheathing my sword in its holder around my waist. "Just focus on me, Ash." I tried to. I wanted to, but the memories haunted my thoughts. Hayley stepped into me and wrapped her arms around my waist, gluing her body to mine. "Just dance with me. Forget about the music; forget about the nymphs. It's just you and me."

You and me.

Me and her.

The warrior and the queen.

My queen.

My mate.

I wound my arms around her, pulling her tight against me. I buried my head in her neck and inhaled deeply, savoring her scent, letting it go to my head, allowing it to erase all other thoughts from my mind. This, this was real. Being here with Hayley. Enjoying her company. Protecting her. Taking care of her. That was what mattered right now and nothing else.

My body relaxed against her, only to stiffen again when I realized how close we were, how her breasts pushed against my chest, how her hips pressed against my thighs.

Slowly, Hayley swayed us side to side again, brushing more of her body against mine.

In the flower's name, she was driving me crazy, and she didn't even know it.

It was futile to fight it. Right now, I had no control. I took in another lungful of her scent and touched my lips to the skin of her neck. Hayley gasped but didn't move away. Instead, she tilted her head, giving me better access.

I lost it. I hadn't touched anyone like this in over fifteen years, and Hayley wasn't just anyone. She was my mate. This moment was more than special, and I couldn't resist anymore. I dragged my lips up her neck, around her jaw, and to her lips. Cupping her face, I brushed my lips over hers. When she didn't pull back, I dove in. I closed my mouth over hers and kissed her.

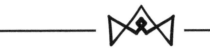

I THOUGHT I WAS DREAMING.

When I saw Ash having what looked like a PTSD episode, I didn't think, I just acted. I embraced him, hoping the contact would ground him and bring him back to the present.

I hadn't expected him to hold me tight, to graze his lips over my neck, for his mouth to find mine.

But I wasn't complaining. This was exactly what I wanted, so when he pressed his lips to mine, I didn't hesitate. I parted my lips for him and let him in. He jumped into me, freefall style. His kiss began slow and deep, but soon it became something more, something desperate, as if I had been the key to his freedom and just now, after fifteen years of bad days, he could escape. He kissed me hard and sensual, taking my breath away.

One of his hands snaked from my face to my nape, while the other splayed on my lower back, keeping me locked in place. As if I was going any other place.

Wanting more of him, needing him, I slid one of my

hands underneath his tunic, feeling his warm skin. I traced his many scars with my fingertips.

Then Ash jumped apart from me.

I frowned. "What's the matter?" His eyes at my feet, he shook his head. Seriously, a warrior as big and as strong as he was would play shy with me right now? Oh, hell no. "Ash, look at me."

"Soldiers!" a nymph yelled. The music died, and the nymphs stopped dancing. "Soldiers are coming this way!"

All business like, Ash put his hand over the hilt of his sword. "What? What do you mean?"

"They come every once in a while to check what we are doing," the spikey-haired nymph said. "I guess they are afraid we'll do something to disrupt Vasant's reign."

"Like bless the real queen," Ash muttered. He stared at me, his green eyes full of concern. The nymphs looked at us, the fear stamped on their faces. "We have to leave."

"There's no time," the nymph who announced the bad news said. "They will be here in ten seconds. They will see you leaving and pursue you."

"Here." The nymph with spiked hair stepped in front of Ash and me. She moved her hand over us, casting a new glamour. My skin tingled as my features seemingly changed. "Now the both of you look like a full-blooded Autumn male and a half-Spring, half-Autumn female." The sounds of horses' hooves reached my ears. "Just act as if you were curious about our ceremonies and wanted to join us."

The music resumed and the nymphs began playing, as if nothing was happening. And Ash stood still by my side as a dozen horses appeared from among the trees. They rode fast until they were a few yards from the hilltop; then they stopped.

One of the soldiers jumped off his horse.

Ash drew in a sharp breath.

"What is it?" I asked, my stomach in knots.

"I know this soldier," Ash muttered, his voice low. "Hinata."

"Enough!" Hinata shouted, his voice echoing over the music. The nymphs stopped playing and dancing and turned to him, faking surprise upon seeing him. "What is going on here?"

The nymph with spiked hair faced him. "We're having one of our ceremonies, as usual."

Hinata's gaze fell on Ash and me. "What about those two?"

"They heard about our famous ceremonies and came to see them for themselves," the nymph said, sounding nonchalant, as if fae came to see the nymphs all the time. I hoped that was the case.

Eyes narrowed, Hinata strode to us. He was not as tall as Ash, but he was wider, with a round chin and short blond hair cut close to his skull. He stared Ash and me down. I clasped my hands behind my back, afraid he would see I was shaking.

"Curious about the floral nymphs, hm?" he asked, his foul breath reaching my nose and making me gag. "What's so special about it?"

"We heard they could perform blessings," Ash said, taking my hand. My eyes went wide for a moment. "You see, my wife and I have been trying to have a baby for years now. We thought we could ask them to bless us so the gods will grant us a child."

What the hell was that? I smoothed my face and offered

Hinata a small smile as I placed my free hand over my stomach. "We really want a family."

Hinata scoffed at us before turning and marching away, walking among the nymphs and looking them up and down, searching for something suspicious. He kicked a few instruments, dropped baskets with food on the ground, drank some of the wine.

Beside me, Ash tensed, his hand tightening around mine. I placed my other hand above our joined fingers and ran my thumb over his skin. I wanted to tell him that everything would be okay, that he just needed to relax and wait. They would leave soon, and we could go on.

But he pulled his hand from mine, his eyes sending a murderous glint at Hinata.

I tried not caring that he had pulled away from me, telling myself that it had been because he was focused on being a warrior right now. It was okay. We had time to talk later and, hopefully, finish what we had started.

Hinata walked back to us and offered me a glass full of wine. "I heard you shouldn't drink when carrying. Drink all you can now."

Shit. I started to bring my trembling hands forward, sure he would see how nervous I was, but Ash was faster. He reached for the glass and grabbed it for me. "Thank you."

Hinata glared at him. "It's for your beautiful wife, not for you." He slapped the glass from Ash's hand, touching Ash in the process.

Ash's glamour broke.

"Ashton," Hinata whispered, his eyes huge.

All hell broke loose. In an instant, Ash and Hinata had their weapons drawn, the nymphs retreated, taking me with them, and the soldiers dismounted and pointed their spears at Ash.

I stepped forward, wanting to help him somehow, but the nymph with spiked hair whispered, "No. They still don't know who you are. You can't get involved."

"And here I thought you had gone to hide in the Summer Court," Hinata said, a nasty smile spreading over his lips. "I believe King Vasant will be very happy when I deliver your head at his feet."

Ash twirled his sword in his hand. "We both know you're no match for me, Hinata."

"But I'm not alone." He gestured to the other eleven soldiers, all ready for battle.

Shit, could Ash fight twelve soldiers at the same time? From what I heard, he had been one of the best warriors in the Spring, but that had been before he was tortured and weakened for fifteen years.

"Are you willing to try?" Ash asked, not one ounce of fear in his voice or his body language.

Hinata answered by raising his sword and lunging at Ash.

I gasped at the loud clank of metal as Ash parried Hinata's attack. A blink of an eye later, Ash kicked Hinata's chest, pushing him back a few feet.

The soldiers advanced on Ash, all at the same time.

And the nymphs ran toward them, weaving through them like leaves in the wind. They danced and sang, spreading their magic and dazing the soldiers.

Ash turned to face me, confused.

"Go," the nymph with spiked hair said. "Though they won't remember much of what happened before the spell, it won't hold for too long. You two better go before they see you again."

Ash marched to me and took my hand.

"Thank you," I said to the nymph as Ash dragged me down the hill.

I LEFT the chalet before the sun rose, jumped on the horse, and rode to the village.

The tug inside my chest only increased with the distance I put between Hayley and me, but it was for the best.

I let out a sigh, remembering last night. Despite our run-in with Hinata and the Spring soldiers, last night had been incredible. I knew I shouldn't have given in, but a part of me didn't regret having held Hayley, having danced with her, having kissed her.

A shiver ran down my spine at the memory of her mouth on mine, of her body pressed against mine. If she hadn't touched my scars and made me self-conscious, I probably would have taken the kiss further than I should have. Holy petals, I shouldn't even have touched her, much less kiss her or more.

During the ride back to the chalet last night, Hayley had tried initiating a conversation, but I only grunted at her, hoping she would get mad at me and shut up. If she kept prodding, if she kept pushing.... I wasn't sure how strong I was when it came to her.

Back at the chalet, I barely looked her way. I went directly to my bedroom and didn't come up for air until this morning, when I woke up before her and fled. I knew Mahaera would come over to train with her in the morning, so I didn't feel too bad about leaving her alone.

Besides being of lowly birth and being told by Mahaere to not act on the mating bond, I couldn't stop thinking about how broken I was. My mind... it wasn't right. I had freaked out when the nymphs played the drums, remembering the horrible sounds I lived with when down in the dungeons— the metal chains echoing in the dark, the saw cutting through flesh, the bone-chilling screams. I had nightmares each time I closed my eyes. All of that meant something wasn't right with me. And it wasn't just the mind stuff. My body was covered in scars. Small ones from hammered nails and slashes to infuse pain, and big ones across my back from being whipped one too many times.

My mind and my body were broken. How could I measure up to Hayley, who was so beautiful, so bright, so perfect? How could I stand by her side while she ruled a country?

She deserved better than me. I would help her take the throne back because this was the last wish her father had made to me before dying, but then... then I wasn't sure what I would do.

With a heavy dark green cloak and hood over myself, I rode into Verdante. I left the horse near the edge of town, where it would be easy to get it from and run away if needed, then walked into the simpler side of the village. The people here looked wary and jumpy.

I walked by two female fae and heard them as they said something about being afraid of the soldiers coming back and searching their females. And now it seemed they were searching the males too.

So, the soldiers were looking for Hayley and me. Had they realized we were together, or did they think it was coincidence?

I entered the tavern at the edge of a dark alley. Despite its foul facade and small interior, the place was organized and smelled of good, sweet food. There were a few customers occupying some tables.

A waitress with a bright yellow dress revealing too much of her plump cleavage smiled at me. "You can sit anywhere you like."

"I'm here to see Nevena," I told her in a low voice.

The waitress looked me up and down, sizing me up. She grunted and pointed to the door in the back. "She's in there."

I marched to the back of the tavern and opened the small wooden door. A busy kitchen greeted me with its heat and sweet scents, and a short, old female fae with messy blonde curls knotted atop of her head commanded the show.

She saw me at the door and dropped the basket of fruit she had in her hands. "General Ashton," she whispered in disbelief. "You ... I heard you were dead."

I gestured at myself. "I'm very much alive."

She rushed to me and gave a tight hug. For such a small female, she was very strong. "Thank the gods." She pulled back and narrowed her eyes at me. "What happened?" I closed the kitchen door and glanced around. She slapped my arm. "We're alone, you fool. You know I don't work with anyone."

I chuckled, even though her slap hadn't been the mildest.

Nevena had been one of the army cooks for many, many years. She had fed all the strong soldiers who fought for King Eden. I had heard she refused to work for the fake king and started working in a crappy tavern. It had been easier to find her than I thought it would be.

While we picked up the dropped fruit, I gave her a summary of the events: about my escape and now my will to get an army together to defeat Vasant, though I didn't tell her anything about Hayley.

She tsked. "You're going to get yourself killed." She mixed chopped vegetables in a pot of boiling water. "Now that you're free, don't you want to live?"

"How can I live in peace knowing my kingdom is being destroyed by the hands of the fake king?" It was an honest response.

Nevena nodded. "I understand. The fake king is a horrible male. May his soul burn into the fiery pits of Uffern." It wasn't often a fae spoke of Uffern, since they were all too afraid of being sent there by the gods once they died. "But tell me, how are you going to find soldiers for this suicide mission?"

"That's why I'm here. I need your help with that."

A string of curses flew from Nevena's mouth. When I thought she would tell me to leave and never come back, she inhaled and asked, "And how do you think I can help?"

"You probably know all the soldiers who survived the war and how I can find them," I told her. "You can even contact them."

She grabbed a sharp knife and pointed it at me. "Listen, General, even if I can contact them, you must know most of them joined the fake king's forces. They were too afraid of what would happen to them or their loved ones if they didn't."

"True, but that doesn't mean they want to serve Vasant." Surrendering to the scents of the kitchen, I snatched a sweet bread roll from a plate. Nevena shook her head at me. "Most of them might just need a push, a reason to fight back. It'll be even better if they are on the inside. It'll make it easier to ambush them when we start this new war."

"War, I hate wars," the old female mumbled.

"Nobody like wars."

She snorted. "Says the soldier who has lived most of his life fighting one."

I sighed. It wasn't most of my life, but a good part of it. "Nevena, please help me. Contact the soldiers you know who were on our side once. See if they still hate Vasant and if they would be willing to fight. Ask them to contact you. I'll do the rest."

The old cook rolled her eyes at me. "You're too pretty for females to say no to, don't you know that?"

I chuckled, remembering her jokes. She used to tease me and a couple of other soldiers, saying we were too pretty to be fighting such a bloody war. I looked down at myself, remembering the hundreds of scars that now marred my body. Even if someday in the past I had been considered pretty, I was sure I wasn't now.

I placed a kiss on the top of her messy bun. "Thank you. I'll be back in a couple of days to check who answered your messages." I turned to leave.

"General," she said with a long sigh. I paused and looked at her. "This war you're planning... it might be too big for just you and a handful of soldiers. If you really want to defeat the fake king, you might have to think of other ways."

I frowned, thinking of what she said. Deep down, I knew I was hoping for too much. Vasant had an army of several thousands of soldiers. How and when would I ever match that? But if not by fighting, how could I take the throne back for Hayley?

"Nevena," I started, the wheels in my mind turning. "Would you be able to send a message to Queen Natsia of the Summer Court and King Cadewyn of the Winter Court?"

Her brows hiked up, but she nodded. "I think so."

I opened my hand to her. "Then give me some paper and ink."

LIKE A FOOL, I waited for Ash all day long. I heard when he left in the early morning, without saying a word to me. In fact, he hadn't said anything or looked my way since we left the Greenarch Hill last night after the soldiers had found him.

And here I thought I had finally broken through the wall that was between us. I wondered... was he like that with all girls or was just me? I wasn't his type, was that it? I mean, I wasn't thinking about the future, about getting married; I just felt a strong connection to him, and he made me feel like mush every time he looked at me. I wanted to melt in his arms while he screwed me senseless.

And yet, after kissing me until I was completely breathless, he simply ignored me.

Thankfully, Mahaera came in the morning and kept me —and my mind—busy with the magic training.

"Just relax," Mahaera said, standing before me outside the chalet. "Your magic is part of you. Embrace it."

First, it took a long time for me to just be able to summon

my magic again, but Mahaera was patient and never reprimanded me. After I was able to feel it, we started by reaching out and sensing the plants around us. Then the ground. The goddess explained that my father could control both plants and earth, and because of that, she was fairly sure I could too.

And she was right. Since I already knew how to sense the plants, it was easy to transfer that same notion to the earth. I could sense it, but I couldn't move it.

"This is useless," I snapped after trying to move one tiny rock for over an hour.

"This is your first day, Hayley," Mahaera said, her voice calm. "Don't despair yet. Soon, you'll be a better magic user than even your father."

I frowned.

My father. I hadn't even known his name until a few days ago, and now I was supposed to be just like him. To inherit his legacy. To be as good as he was. Or better.

"I need a break," I muttered.

Mahaera didn't push as I sat down on the porch steps and drank water for over ten minutes. But that was how long I needed to clear my mind, to calm my feelings, so I could continue.

We practiced for another hour, until finally I moved the damn rock.

"See?" Mahaera smiled at me. "I knew you could do it."

We went back to the top. Feeling the plants, trying to move the leaves and petals all around us. Feeling the earth, trying to move the rocks.

By late afternoon, I was dead on my feet. Mahaera sent me back inside the chalet, telling me to go take a bath and rest.

I did that, but like a bigger fool, I also made dinner, or

supper as Ash called it, thinking he would arrive back at any moment and at least eat with me. But he was avoiding me. That was crystal clear.

Why though? Was it because of the kiss? I mean, it had been an earth-shattering kiss that I felt deep in my core. Hadn't he felt that too? Didn't he want to repeat it? Didn't he want to see where it took us? How great going further could be?

My stomach tightened with embarrassment. Shit, perhaps that was exactly why he was avoiding me, because it had been horrible for him. And as his queen—ugh, I hated him calling me that—now he didn't know how to look me in the eye. He always treated me with so much respect and composure, and after a moment of weakness, he did something he hadn't planned to, that he didn't want to.

Wanting to disappear into a hole deep in the earth, I cleaned up the kitchen, put away the rest of the food, and went to my bedroom, where I changed into a loose tunic Mahaera had brought for me, which was the only thing that resembled pajamas. Then I crawled into bed and willed sleep to come.

Instead, I heard movement a few minutes later. On my tiptoes, I went to the door, rested my ear on the wood, and listened. I told myself I just did that to make sure it was Ash and not someone else invading the chalet.

The faint footsteps paused in front of my door, but only for a brief moment. Then he went on to his bedroom and closed the door with a soft click.

Prick. Bastard. Jerk.

Wasn't he man enough to continue what he had started? That kiss hadn't been a simple kiss. It had implied sex, plain and simple. Holy shit, sex with him. Just the thought of being under his rock-hard body made me feel hot all over.

With a grunt, I went back to bed, closed my eyes, and counted sheep so I wouldn't think of the warrior in the bedroom across the hallway.

I restarted my sheep counting hundreds of times in the next hour or so. I wasn't even sure what time it was anymore, but one thing I was sure of: I wasn't going to be able to sleep if I didn't calm down somehow.

In need of some water to help reduce my body heat, I tiptoed out of my bedroom, heading for the kitchen.

Then I heard it. A thump sound and groans. I knew these sounds. I had heard them before.

Without hesitation, I entered Ash's bedroom. Dim light from the moon filtered through the half-opened curtains, showing me the man on the floor, jerking around every few seconds, bumping his body on the hardwood and grunting as nightmares tormented him.

This time I knew better than get too close to wake him up. Well, not that I minded being under him, but last time, he thought I was an enemy and he could have hurt me.

So I grabbed a pillow from his bed and threw it at him. "Ash, wake up!" He jerked again but didn't wake up. I got closer and poked his side with my foot. "Wake up, damn it!" I poked him hard.

Ash made a swipe for my foot, but I pulled back before he could snatch it. Then he jumped to his feet in a beautiful kick up, his legs apart and slightly bent and his hands in front of himself, ready for battle.

He saw it was me, and his eyes widened, his shoulders relaxing. Straightening, he said, "My queen."

I fought an eye roll. Why was he calling me that again? I let out a sigh. "I think you were having a nightmare again."

Ash lowered his head and took a step back. I felt mad at the gesture. What? Was he afraid I was going to jump on him? But by retreating, he positioned himself right in front of the moonlight coming from the window. I gulped as I took him in. Wearing only brown pants, his sculpted torso, shoulders, and arms were visible. He had mentioned before that, for fifteen years, he had barely exercised, but somehow his body was still made of pure muscle. If he was like this now, how big and powerful had he been before?

Before I could stop it, my mind flew from me. I imagined those arms around me, holding me tight while he made love to me. Heat spread over my body.

Ash reached for a tunic over his bed. I moved before I gave any thought to it. I stepped forward and blocked his arm, keeping his shirt away.

"What are you doing?" he asked, his voice low.

I reached up and traced the outline of several small scars across his chest. "Are these part of your nightmares?"

"My queen...." He sucked in a sharp breath as I slid my fingers lower, to the scars on his abdomen. "I would rather you not see my scars."

"Why?" I brought my other hand up and continued touching him, caressing the marks that added to his torment. "They are part of you. They make General Ashton stronger and more powerful. More badass."

He scoffed. "No. They bring me painful memories and make me self-conscious of how broken I am."

My fingers paused, and I looked up at him. My heart squeezed at his sudden confession. He thought he was broken? Every one of us was a little broken. All you had to do was find the missing piece that would fit your broken frame. And for some reason, I liked to think he was mine. After all, this feeling, this pull I felt toward him couldn't be just attraction, could it?

There was only one way to find out.

I traced my fingertips lower.

"My queen," he said with a groan. "Please, stop touching me."

"Why?" I asked in a whisper.

"Because... it's hard fighting my self-control."

I stilled. Wait. So, he wanted me too and he was trying not to give in? Why? Well, I didn't care about the reason at that exact moment. I rose to my tiptoes, leaning into him, and whispered, "Who says I want you to hold on to your self-control?"

Closing his eyes, he shook his head.

Too bad. I was going to make him lose his self-control right now.

Feeling bold and empowered, I quickly slipped my hand under his pants and closed my palm around his cock, already hard and hot.

"My queen, no," he whispered, taking a step back and bumping into the wall.

I moved with him, not letting go of him. "Why not?" I moved my hand up and down his length, pushing hard against the hilt, creating a delicious friction I knew he couldn't resist.

"Because...." His breath caught, and he gritted his teeth. I kept pumping my hand over him, loving the sight of him leaning against the wall, closing his eyes, his mouth open, as he started losing his self-control. "Hayley...." He groaned as his body shuddered.

"Just give in," I whispered, placing a soft kiss on his chin. "Give in to me."

He groaned again but didn't push me back. He didn't tell me to stop.

I took that as permission to keep going. With a small smile, I knelt in front of him, lowered his pants, and paused for a brief second. Holy shit, I had felt he was big, but now, being face-to-face with his cock, I was speechless. A shiver rolled down my spine imagining him inside me....

No, that was for later. For now, I licked the tip of his cock while tightening my hand around him.

"For leaves' sake," he whispered.

I played with him for a moment, licking his length, swirling my tongue on the tip, pressing hard with my hand, increasing the pressure.

Then I took him in my mouth.

Ash let out a growl as his body trembled. I didn't think he knew what he was doing when he knotted his fingers in my hair and gently tugged me forward. I smiled, even with his cock filling my mouth, and started moving back and forth, back and forth, taking as much of him as I could. His breathing grew ragged and heavy—music to my ears. This was a first, having Ash this disarmed and undone in front of me.

I liked him like this... but just for me.

I traced my hand over the hard muscles of his legs, grazing my nails on the sensitive spot on the inside of his thighs.

"Hayley," he whispered as his body trembled. His hands tightened around my head, pulling me closer. "In the flower's name...."

I moved faster and pressed my lips harder, knowing what

that meant. A moment later, hot liquid spilled into my mouth. I swallowed, licked his cock one more time, and glanced up.

Ash's body trembled once more, and he took a deep breath.

Then he looked down at me.

I thought I was in trouble until he hooked his hands under my arm, pulled me up, and twisted us around, pushing me against the wall. His hands on my wrists, he held my arms by the sides of my head.

He leaned into me. "Do you have any idea what you just did to me?" His voice was rough and breathy, and his green eyes shone with pure desire.

Desire for me.

"Hm, if you're not sure, I can repeat it," I joked, loving this moment, loving how close he was, how he was looking at me.

"I haven't...." He pressed his lips together and shook his head.

All right, this was enough. He was thinking too much, and soon he would break this spell. I didn't want him to. I knew he felt the same as me. I knew it. He just had to give in.

I placed my hand over his fast-beating heart and rose to my tiptoes, getting closer to him. "Just kiss me already."

Ash let out a growl.

Then his mouth crashed onto mine. He pressed his body against mine, locking me between him and the wall. And I melted into him. His lips were soft as they moved against mine in a frantic rhythm, as if he couldn't get enough of this. Of me.

That feeling, that knowledge, made me even bolder. I wound my arms around his neck and hooked my legs on his waist. Hands clutching my ass, Ash deepened the kiss and glued his body to mine. I gasped against his mouth as his erection rubbed at my hips. He was already hard again? How the hell? Did fae have more stamina and energy than humans? Damn, I hoped so, because if he didn't take me soon, I would die.

I almost cheered when Ash held my entire weight in his arms and carried me to his bed. He broke the kiss to lay me down on the mattress, his eyes fixed on mine, shining with so much want, my insides knotted in anticipation. He crawled over me and—

He went completely still.

No, no, he couldn't stop now. I reached for him, but Ash left the bed and put a finger over his lips.

I sat up. "What?"

His brow furrowed. "We aren't alone."

I CURSED myself as I picked up my pants and a tunic from the bed, quickly shoved them on, and reached for my sword on the floor, beside my sleeping spot.

In the middle of the bed, with her legs completely exposed because of the blooming tunic, Hayley watched me, her eyes huge, her face pale.

For leaves' sake, I had almost slept with her. I had almost taken my queen, my mate, to bed, even though I had promised Mahaera I wouldn't act on the mating bond until later—if I ever did it.

But when Hayley came to me, when she was the only one that could send the nightmares away, when she touched my scars, not disgusted by them, when she started it all and gave me the best blow job of my life... how could I resist? I liked to think I was a strong warrior. But when it came to her, I wasn't. If she asked me, I would take her.

Just not right here, not right now.

"What do you mean we're not alone?" Hayley asked, her voice low.

I placed my finger overs my lips again.

It had probably been luck, but I had heard a faint creak from a loose board on the front porch. With my fae hearing, that should have been easy to hear, but I had been so focused on Hayley, I almost missed it.

I didn't know who was outside or how many they were, but one thing I was sure: if they were sneaking around the chalet in the middle of the night, then they weren't friends.

I grabbed Hayley's hand and dragged her out of the bed. "Listen to me," I said in a low voice. "Depending on who it is, we won't be able to get out of here without fighting. If that happens, I want you to be out of the way, okay? Hide somewhere and wait until it's all clear."

Her brows curled down. "I trained with Mahaera today. I can try using my magic."

I shook my head. "You'll need more than just one day of practice to be able to join a real fight."

She glared at me. "Ash, I—"

I placed my finger over her lips, silencing her. The front door had just been opened, and faint footsteps entered the chalet. "They are here," I mouthed to her, not daring to say or whisper anything. My heart hammered, worried about Hayley. The last thing I needed was to involve her in a battle when she wasn't ready for that yet.

Stepping in front of her, I faced the door, my sword ready at my hand.

The door flew open and vines burst in, coming directly for us. I quickly channeled my magic and stopped a few of them, then slashed through the rest.

By then soldiers in green and golden uniforms ran into the bedroom, forming a circle around Hayley and me, their weapons pointed at us. I reached back, snatched Hayley's wrist, and pulled her closer to me.

Eight. There were eight soldiers. If I coordinated it right, I could fight through them all, and we could escape.

"I hoped this would be easier."

I looked at the door just as a figure walked in.

Ilan.

Realization hit me hard in the gut. "You... you did this?"

He halted in the circle with his soldiers. "I came for your head, but I never expected I would find a bigger reward." He shifted his gaze to Hayley. "King Eden's daughter. King Vasant's been looking for her everywhere."

I tightened my grip around Hayley's wrist. "Why? I thought you hated Vasant. I thought you wanted to join me."

Ilan let out a long sigh. "I do hate Vasant, and I do want to join you, but face it, Ash, you're fighting a losing war. You can't win against Vasant. Are you stupid? You really think you can get an army together and reignite a war just like that? Even if you find soldiers willing to join you, that process will be slow. It'll take years, holy petals, decades for you to have an army that measures up to Vasant's forces."

I shook my head. "You don't know that. Once I have a good number on my side, I'll publicly look for soldiers. Many will desert Vasant to join us."

"Have you any idea how afraid everyone is of Vasant?" Ilan asked, his eyes narrowed. "Even by just speaking his name, I feel like shuddering. No one will dare go against the king."

"Fake king," I said through gritted teeth.

"You can call him whatever you want. It won't change the fact that he's the one sitting on the throne and running this kingdom."

"You mean destroying this kingdom."

Ilan shrugged. "Well, it's the price to pay. And once I deliver your head to Vasant, along with Eden's daughter, Vasant will honor me. My future and my family's will be secured."

I felt sick to my stomach. General Ilan had been such a great warrior, with honor for a last name. And now he was selling me out and taking Hayley for his own gain?

He disgusted me.

And he talked too much.

Ready to end this, I let go of Hayley and attacked. Two were down before any of the others reacted. I went next for Ilan, but he stepped back, the coward. Three soldiers engaged me at once, and I did some real dancing with them.

I focused on my fight—jabbing, twirling, parrying, dodging—and tried not to think about Hayley. By now, she was probably being held by soldiers, but I knew they wouldn't hurt her. She was too valuable. Vasant would want to play with her before actually killing her.

That thought filled me with rage.

A soldier came at me, pushing his sword forward. I leaned to the side, bringing my sword up and bumping his out of the way. Before he could bring it back down again, I quickly slashed across his chest.

His body fell at my feet.

I lost the battle against my worry and glanced at Hayley. She jerked against the hold of two soldiers, while another one stood in front of her, just watching her. Then she closed her eyes and I felt it. Her magic brushing against me. I thought I had sensed it because, as her mate, her magic spoke to me, because the soldier didn't react to it. So they were startled when vines surged from outside, breaking the glass window into a million shards. The vines quickly wrapped around the three soldiers, freeing Hayley. The soldiers fought against the vines, but Hayley held on to her power, keeping them in place.

A corner of my lips tugged up as pride filled my chest.

Hayley picked up a spear from the floor and stared at it for a minute. She tentatively aimed the weapon at a soldier's chest.

Then she shook her head and dropped the weapon.

I could do it for her.

I stopped playing with the soldiers I was fighting. I kicked the side of one, destabilizing him, and ran my sword through his throat. Another one came at me, but I was ready for him. I sidestepped him, swinging my sword up and slashing across his chest.

Knowing I had cut through critical veins and they would soon bleed out, I didn't finish it right away. I looked up, searching for Ilan, but he had disappeared.

Truly a coward.

I stepped back and went to Hayley. "Close your eyes," I told her. She pressed her eyes shut, and I quickly stabbed a soldier through the heart. He died instantly.

I was ready to stab another when a yelp echoed behind me.

I turned.

A few steps from me, Ilan held Hayley with his sword poised at her neck. "Drop your weapon or she dies."

Even though I knew he wouldn't kill her, I didn't want him to hurt her in any way. My heart pounded hard in apprehension as I lowered my sword to the floor and raised my hands over my head.

"You'll be very sorry for this," Hayley said. She wiggled

her fingers, and the vines holding the remaining two soldiers grew further, surging forward to Ilan. They came at him like a ton of bricks and knocked him back.

Ilan lost the grip on his sword as he fell on his butt a few feet from Hayley. And I didn't waste time. I picked my sword up and advanced on him, plunging my blade into his chest.

"I'm sorry it has to be this way," I whispered as he closed his eyes and left this world.

I turned to the other soldiers. If I was right, Ilan had come here to get me. Apparently, General Xuan hadn't spread the news that Hayley was with me. Without another word, I approached the whimpering soldiers and ended their lives as painlessly as I could.

My shoulders sagged.

I had just killed a male I had called my friend for most of my life, and this place that I had always considered a safe haven was compromised.

With a sigh, I turned to Hayley. She was even paler now, her eyes wide as she took in the nine bodies at our feet.

I went to her, cupped her face, and forced her to look at me. "Hey, are you okay?" A thin scratch marred the skin of her neck, where Ilan's sword had pressed against her throat. Rage coiled in my stomach, but I did my best to keep it in. She had gone through enough just now.

Slowly, she nodded. "I-I will be, I think."

"Then go pack." I dropped my hand from her face. "We're leaving."

ASH GAVE me ten minutes to grab my things, which weren't many, get some food, and meet him outside by the horse. My movements were automatic, and my mind was numb as I went through the motions.

When we were finally on the horse's back and riding away from the chalet in the middle of the night, I inhaled deeply, taking in the pine and oak scents from the forest and letting them clear my thoughts.

Besides having just started a great night with Ash and finally broken through his wall, we also had a nasty fight, and he had to kill nine fae soldiers, one of which seemed to be a friend of his.

Knowing he probably had much to think about, I just wound my arms around his waist and rested my cheek on his shoulder blade, giving him some kind of support.

"Do you want to talk about it?" I whispered after we had been on the road for over one hour.

Ash shrugged. "Talk about the fact that I killed a fae who

had fought beside me? Who helped me lead your father's army?"

I hugged him tighter. "I'm sorry." That wasn't the only topic I would like to discuss, but we could start with the battle, sure. "I'm sorry he betrayed you."

"I'm starting to wonder if he's right," Ash muttered. "If everyone is so afraid of Vasant, won't they all betray me?"

"You can't think like that; otherwise you won't go through with your plan."

What the hell was I saying? Wasn't I the one who still had doubts about his entire plan? But how was I supposed to have faith in it and want it and fight for it when he didn't? I needed him to be strong and sure, so I could become like that one day. I still wasn't sure about being a queen and leading the kingdom, but I could definitely help him take the court back. Later we would find someone worthy to rule.

Ash let out a long breath. "Just... hang tight. This will be a long ride."

I took that as a sign to shut my mouth and let him mourn in his own way.

In the dark of the night, we rode through the forest, coasting around a quiet, desolate village. It broke my heart to see so much decaying and suffering, such a big contrast from Verdante.

Then as the sun rose, we cut through the outskirts of another village. Shouts and crying reached our ears. I brushed sleep away, and Ash slowed the horse down.

"What's going on?" I asked, looking down the main street but not seeing much.

"I don't know," Ash said, also watching the area.

A piercing scream brought shivers to my arms. Without a

word, Ash steered the horse deeper into the village. Loud voices and more shouts welcomed us as we hopped off the horse and slowly approached the commotion. Near the village's center, soldiers stood in a circle, turned to the outside, pushing back the yelling fae who tried to break through the barrier.

"Stay back!" a soldier shouted, pushing an elderly male. He fell on his back but was quickly aided by others.

"What the hell?" I muttered.

"Look." Ash jerked his chin forward.

A woman stepped over a makeshift dais. The first thing that shocked me was that she wasn't from the Spring Court as she had messy black hair and dark eyes. Then I realized she also wasn't fae as her ears weren't pointed.

But what shocked me the most was that she tugged on a rope and a line of young female fae with their wrists bound to the rope scrambled over the dais, all of them crying and begging to be let go.

All of them just like me.

My stomach dropped.

"Who's she?" I asked in a low voice.

"Sanna," Ash whispered. "Vasant's woman and his most powerful weapon."

I frowned, trying to remember where I had heard her name before.

"I know you've been harboring an enemy," the woman said, her voice gruff and crisp. She tugged on the rope again, and the young fae fell to their knees, one on top of the other. The other fae screamed in rage. "And I think the enemy is one of these females." She lifted her hand in front of her face and slowly closed her fingers. The young fae gasped and choked, all of them trying to claw at their necks with their bound hands. Oh, she was the witch who worked for Vasant. "Tell me which one, and I'll let the others live!"

The crowd shouted, saying that their daughters, sisters, and wives weren't the one the woman was looking for.

"Let them go!" the elderly male from before screamed.

"You'll keep insisting none of these is the enemy?" the witch asked. Pressing her lips tight, she let go of her magic. The young fae gasped as they tried to catch their breaths. But the woman wasn't done. She grabbed the hair of the nearest fae and pulled up. "You asked for this." She placed her hand over the fae's chest. The young fae's eyes rolled back. Sanna let her go, and her body fell back on top the other fae. Screams rang louder. "Next!" the woman said, taking another one by the hair.

I felt sick to my stomach.

I took a step forward.

Ash's hand closed around my wrist. He tugged me back around a corner. "What are you doing?"

"I... I don't know." A lump formed in my throat. "I just can't watch that. That girl just died because of me. I can't let that happen again." My eyes itched as tears blurred my vision. "I can't be responsible for so many deaths. I need to turn myself in."

Ash's nostrils flared as he exhaled. "Believe me, I feel as sick as you do, but if you turn yourself in, everything is over. Vasant will have won. He'll continue to be king, and the people will continue to suffer." His thumb ran the inside of my wrist. "Hayley, I understand, and I'm so glad to see you caring, because these are not just random people. These are *your* people, and only you can save them. But not here, not now." He let go of my wrist, placing a firm hand on my lower back. "Come on." He gently pushed me away from the commotion.

Away from the murders.

I wiped at my eyes. "I understand your reasoning, but it's hard." My steps were slow and reluctant. "How am I supposed to sleep in peace knowing these girls are dying for me?"

"You're not supposed to sleep in peace," Ash said. I glared at him, but before I could say anything, he went on. "Because if you can't sleep in peace, then it means you need to do something to make it better, to one day be able to sleep in peace." We arrived back at the horse, and Ash mounted up. "Once you're on the throne, we'll be able to fix everything." He offered me his hand and helped me up behind him. "And we'll make everything better."

Ash kicked the sides of the horse and away we went, leaving the village and the young fae who were dying in my stead behind. New tears sprouted in my eyes—I didn't think I would ever be able to think about this and not cry.

As we rode away, I tried thinking about what all of this meant.

Ash was right. I did care. I cared too much. I wanted to help everyone, to save every single fae in the Spring Court. I didn't care about the throne and being queen, but if that was the only way for me to be able to help the fae and make their lives better, then so be it.

I would become the damn queen.

My chest tightened with my new decision, and a wave of apprehension fell over me. Certainly, kicking Vasant from the throne and becoming queen wasn't going to be an easy task. Or fast.

But with Ash by my side, guiding my steps and helping me, I was sure I could do it.

After an hour of riding through the forest, we arrived at another small village, Cheerville. We skirted it at first, but then Ash steered the horse toward it.

"What are you doing?" I asked, worried. I didn't want to see any more fae suffering. Yes, I wanted to help them, but I might break down from sadness and despair if I kept seeing the terrors of Vasant's reign before I could actually take measures into my own hands.

"We barely slept last night, and before that you spent the entire day training. You must be exhausted." True, but that didn't mean I wanted to be seen by anyone. "This is supposed to be one of the worst villages in the Spring Court," Ash continued. "Most fae already abandoned it. I think it's safe to say soldiers won't be around, and you should be fine, at least until tomorrow."

Ash brought the horse into the village, and my heart broke some more upon seeing how desolate this placed looked. Like the two previous towns we had seen, this one was dark, the colors faded. The buildings and houses seemed abandoned, the streets were littered with trash and rotting food. The plants were dying or already dead. And the few fae around looked too weak and sick to stand up straight.

We stopped at the side of an inn, and Ash left the horse with a young stable boy who desperately needed another meal. Inside the inn, dust gathered in every corner and cockroaches crawled across the floor.

I yelped when one ran just by my feet.

"Ash, I don't think I'll be able to sleep here," I whispered.

Ignoring me, he talked to the lady behind the counter. A

few seconds later, she handed him a key and pointed to the stairs behind us.

As we went up the stairs, Ash said, "I know it looks bad, but that makes this place even safer to stay."

Ugh, I thought I preferred sleeping in the forest than here.

Surprisingly, the room wasn't so bad. A low, queen bed with mostly clean covers was to one side, an armchair and round table on the other with a lit lantern on top of it. The curtains and the small rug on the floor needed a good wash, but other than that, it seemed okay. At least, I hadn't seen any cockroaches in here yet.

After taking turns in the small bathroom to wash up, Ash lay down on the dusty rug, his back to the bed.

I stared at him, lost. Hm, he was just going to stay there, on the hard floor, after everything we did at his chalet the previous night? I got it, we were both exhausted. I wasn't asking for him to jump on me right now, but he could at least lie down beside me and hold me while we slept, right?

"Um, the bed is big enough," I said, feeling a little self-conscious. "You can sleep here." *With me*, I wanted to add but held my tongue.

"No, it's fine," Ash muttered, not moving an inch or looking at me. "I prefer the floor."

I frowned. Was that his way of dismissing me? What was I to him? Just his damn queen? A woman he kissed sometimes when he was feeling vulnerable? Neither?

Shame and rage filled my veins, but I contained all the curses that sprouted to my tongue. Suddenly, I wanted to send this whole plan to hell. Why was I supposed to help him and follow his damn plan when he purposely ignored me?

New tears brimmed in my eyes, but these ones were of

shame. I shouldn't have said anything. In fact, I should have been faster and taken the bed before he lay down on the floor, then told him to go sleep somewhere else.

Defeated, I dragged my butt to the bed, rested my head on the foul-smelling pillow, and pretended to fall asleep in two seconds flat.

IT WAS TOO HARD STAYING beside Hayley all the time and not going to her, not touching her, not telling her how I truly felt. So in the mornings, I got up before her and left the inn when Mahaera arrived for their training session.

The goddess hadn't said anything, but even she, the most kind and gentle of them all, had glared at me the day after we fled the chalet. Did the goddesses know everything? Didn't we have any kind of privacy? Thankfully, she hadn't grilled me about it, probably because she knew I would do my best to keep my promise from now on.

Hayley hadn't said much either, though I wasn't sure if it was because I barely saw her or because she was mad at me. I knew she was mad at me. I could feel her rage rolling in waves, directed at me, like a tangible tsunami. Soon, I would drown in it.

The first day, I walked around the village, checking everything out—all the fae, all the buildings, all the corners. I wanted to make sure that there were no hidden soldiers waiting to attack, or that we could flee easily in case they suddenly came this way.

The second day, I made an actual list of the fae still living at the village, hoping that I would find a few young fae fit to join an army. But my hope was short-lived, because everyone in this place was malnourished. Maybe if I bought them a few meals, they would gain enough strength to start training. But then what? The other fae would hear about that and want meals too. Or they would want me to do more. Word would spread, and soon Vasant would hear about a former general who was offering meals to any fae willing to join his army.

It would be a disaster.

On the third day, I patrolled the village's perimeter. Things were getting too slow, and I was running out of things to do. Besides, it was getting harder and harder to leave Hayley in the mornings and to see her pretending to be sleeping when I got back at night.

On the fourth day, I finally had something to do. Trusting Hayley to Mahaera, I rode the horse back to Verdante to meet with Nevena. It had been a week since I last met her. She should have some news for me by now.

Careful with soldiers and other curious fae, I slipped into town and into the tavern where Nevena worked. As expected, she was at the kitchen, cooking away like no one's business.

"Any news for me?" I asked as I went in.

"Your mother was a very kind fae, General Ashton, and your father upheld honor and respect the most," she said as she chopped carrots with a sharp knife. She stopped and glanced at me. "How come you arrive here and don't say hello and ask how am I?"

One corner of my lips curled up. "Good morning, Nevena. How are you?"

She rolled her eyes. "Too late, my boy. Too late." She waved the knife to a drawer in the corner before continuing chopping the vegetables. "I've got some letters for you in there."

Holding my breath, I opened the drawer and got the thin stack of letters. There were only thirteen, but when I read them, the notes mentioned more than one or two names. In total, I had just acquired forty-six soldiers. Leif and Gul sent me a note too. They mentioned finding out Ilan had betrayed me and led soldiers to my chalet. Now I was in hiding because of that, and the fake king had doubled the soldiers combing through the villages, both for me and for some half-fae, half-human female he seemed obsessed about.

So not even the soldiers knew who Hayley was. Just that this female needed to be found.

"No news from the Summer or Winter Courts?" I asked, skimming through the notes again.

Not taking her eyes from her cutting board and now the beets she was cutting, Nevena shook her head. "Nothing."

Well, at least I had received some notes. After Ilan betrayed me, I thought I wouldn't receive any.

I took my time writing back to all the soldiers, telling them that soon I would send word of a meeting time and place. We needed to meet to talk about some details before moving forward.

I asked Nevena to send those letters for me, thanked her profusely, grabbed a sweet roll from the basket, and left as she cursed at me for ruining her day.

As I made my way back to the Greenway, the exhilaration I felt when I saw those thirteen notes slowly deflated. What was forty something soldiers against tens of thousands?

This was a blooming joke. If we were to start a war and win, preferably sooner rather than later, we needed more. But what? I hadn't heard back from the Summer Queen or the Winter King yet, and they were my only other hope. Knowing they hated Vasant as much as I did, I had asked for their support, in any way they could give it to me. Queen Natsia had already expressed her reluctance in participating in a new war, but if she could send me some weapons, horses, or even some torn uniforms, it would be a big help.

I took my time going back to Cheerville, which was a war inside my own heart. I wanted to hurry and see Hayley, make sure she was okay, but at the same time, I shouldn't. I couldn't.

I arrived back too early, so I stayed in the lower level of the inn, where a small tavern was located, seated in a dark corner and drinking a glass of mild ale. I had argued with myself because a soldier shouldn't drink on duty, but right then I just needed a sip to help me relax.

Not long after, a waitress halted beside my table. "Here." She handed me a folded paper.

Brow furrowed, I took the paper from her, unfolded it, and read it.

Come to the room.

—M.

I finished my ale in one long swallow and dragged my feet upstairs. I lifted my hand to knock on the door, but Mahaera opened it before I could.

"Come in," she said, her voice sweet.

I didn't look at Hayley as I entered the room, but the pull in my chest grew stronger. I didn't understand it. Sometimes it was stronger when I was close, and sometimes it was stronger when I was far away. Either way, it was always present, reminding me that she was my mate and that would never change.

"How is training going?" I asked Mahaera.

The goddess showed me a closed-lip smile. "It's going well. Hayley is getting stronger every day. Soon, she'll be more powerful than you are." Which was good news. If she was supposed to rule a kingdom, she should be the strongest there was. "But I didn't call you to talk about training." She extended her hand to me, and a yellow envelope appeared in her palm. "This is for you."

So many blooming notes today. With a sigh, I took the envelope and fished the folded yellow paper from inside. Written in golden ink, the letter was from Queen Natsia.

I frowned. "Why do you have this?" I had sent word by Nevena. I thought that if I got an answer, it would have been through her too.

"Let's say I wanted to speed up things," Mahaera said as if this were explanation enough. Seeing as she was a goddess, I let it go. "You don't need to read the letter. I'll tell you about it." I lowered the paper and watched the goddess. "In a few days, Vasant will throw a ball to celebrate fifteen years of his reign."

Fifteen years since he had killed my king and his family and captured me.

My stomach twisted as old memories and feeling flooded my mind and chest. "And?" I asked through gritted teeth.

"Even though Vasant always invites all the royals of Wyth to any of his parties and ceremonies, they all refuse to come," Mahaera said. "But this time, Natsia and Cadewyn are willing to go. They also talked to King Altan and Queen Zora of the Dawn Court, and they are willing to come too."

I shook my head. "Why?"

She offered yet another envelope, but a bright green one this time. "Because you both will go too. During this ball, you'll start the war."

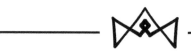

THE PLAN WAS SET in motion. All we had to do now was wait. Well, I kept on practicing with Mahaera, and Ash ran around trying to find more soldiers he could trust—a hard task for such a short time.

If up to Ash, I would spend the days locked in that trashy inn, practicing and hiding. But every time I glanced out the window, I saw the people of this village starving and sick, and it broke my heart.

So, one day before the ball, I got a bunch of supplies—ingredients for a hearty soup and medicine for all kinds of ailments—and set up a small stand at the center of the village, all with Mahaera's help. At first, the people were wary of what I was doing. Mahaera was beside me, though she had a glamour on so no one recognized her for what she was. She urged me not to give up.

A mother with a toddler and a baby dragged their feet nearby, the three of them hacking up coughs that grated at my ears. I didn't give them a chance to turn me down. I grabbed the toddler in my arms, snatched the mother's wrist, and pulled them to the stand. Under the mother's watchful eyes, I cleaned the children's hands and face, fed them the soup, and gave them some medicine. When she realized I was helping without expecting anything back, she let me do the same for her.

Once the trio was done, a line started forming in front of my stand. In a couple of hours, I had fed and treated over forty fae. They thanked me profusely and went on, spreading the word about what I was doing. I just asked them to tell their friends, but no one else. There weren't any soldiers left in this village, but one could never be too careful.

The sun was starting its slow descent down the horizon when Mahaera said she had to leave.

"I'm guessing you can finish up here by yourself, right?" she said, walking away.

I opened my mouth to protest, but I was busy cleaning up a child's scraped knee; otherwise, I would have held on to her and asked her to stay. With a sigh, I finished working on the child and gave his entire family bowls of soup.

I glanced in the big pot. I had already cooked more soup three times. Soon, it would all be gone again. But since it was getting dark, I would close up shop when this batch finished. If some fae complained, I would promise to come back the next day.

I was handing out bowls of soup to an elderly couple when I saw Ash walking down the street toward my stand. I braced myself, knowing he would yell at me, pack my things, and drag me inside the inn. Ugh, he would probably assign one of his new soldiers to keep guard at our room's door so I couldn't leave anymore.

Instead, he halted by my side, snatched the ladle from my

hand, and helped me serve the last of the soup to a father and two young fae.

"Thank you," the father said before ushering his sons away.

There were still a handful of fae in line, but by now it was getting dark and the food was gone.

"I'm sorry, but we need to get going," Ash said, his voice loud and clear. "We'll be back tomorrow."

"You promise?" someone asked from the line, her voice trembling.

"We promise," Ash said with a half smile.

My heart tugged. He hadn't smiled at me, not even once, but he gave free half smiles to the fae of the Spring Court.

The fae dispersed, and Ash started collecting the things Mahaera had helped me acquire. I watched him for a moment, confused about his actions.

"Why aren't you yelling at me?" I finally asked.

"Though I would rather you stay inside, I understand why you wanted to do this." Ash stopped and looked at me. "And I like it. Once more, you're showing me you care about your people." He picked up the empty pot from the stand. "You'll be a great queen."

I didn't know if I should feel proud of his compliment or annoyed. He'd been avoiding me since that night we had to flee his chalet, but there were a handful of moments, like this one, when he said something nice that tugged at my heart.

Why was he doing this to me?

In silence, Ash and I took the stand and everything else inside.

The inn owner stopped us at the stairs. "What the blossom do you think you're doing? Giving away food right in front of my tavern? Do you think that is good for business?"

With a sigh, Ash dropped the things he was carrying, reached into his pocket, and grabbed a few gold coins. He handed them to the owner. "Is this enough to make you shut up about it?"

The owner's eyes went wide. "Oh, why, yes. Keep selling soup and whatever else you want to." He shuffled away, his eyes glued to the coins in his hands.

I wanted to say something, like thank you or tell him he shouldn't have done that, but Ash picked up the stuff from the stairs and carried on, as if I wasn't standing right by his side.

This ignoring thing was really getting the best of me. At first, I was mad about it, but now I just felt sad. Defeated. If there was another way, I would ask Mahaera to take me with her to wherever she lived instead of staying in this tiny, crappy room with the man who made my heart beat faster.

Inside the bedroom, I realized it was past supper time, but the soup was gone. There was no more food. "Hm, are you hungry? Do you want me to make you more soup?"

Ash put all the things away in a corner of the room and turned to me. "No, I'm good. Thank you, my queen."

I flinched. Here he was, calling me my queen again.

Upset, I sat on the windowsill and glanced out to the darkening skies, trying to clear my mind before I said something I didn't mean to. I didn't move from that spot for a long time. Meanwhile, Ash washed up in the bathroom, then doused the lights, and settled down on the rug.

I didn't think I could sleep, not knowing tomorrow was the big day. We were going to willingly enter the Evergreen Palace. I would come face-to-face with Vasant. And we would start a war.

When the moon was high in the sky, Ash sat up on the floor. "I guess neither of us will be able to sleep tonight."

I scoffed. "You think?"

Ash shot up to his feet. "Let's go for a ride."

I frowned. "What? Now?"

He shrugged. "Why not? You won't sleep, will you? This way we at least do something, try to relax, and think of other things."

Like what? Going for a ride with him meant I had to sit with him on the horse, my chest glued to his back, my hands around him. I wasn't so sure that was a good idea.

But he was throwing me a rope here. Even if it was just a peace gesture to try and lessen the heavy mood hanging around us lately, I had to take it.

I stood from the windowsill. "All right."

In no time, we were riding away from the village, deeper into the forest. The air was pleasantly cool, with strong scents of oak and sweet flowers. But what I really liked about the ride was the colors. The greens were so bright the different shades could be seen in detail, and the flowers glowed pink, yellow, orange. It seemed like we had stepped into a futuristic world where aliens lived.

Well, maybe fae were like aliens in that sense, living in their own magical world.

Ash brought the horse to a stop when we arrived at a stunning meadow. I gasped as I glanced around, taking in all the different colors. Flowers of all sizes and shapes and colors —pink, yellow, orange, blue, purple, red, and more, so much more.

Ash helped me jump down from the horse, and I mindlessly walked among the flowers, touching their petals, feelings their different textures, smelling their different scents.

The flowers moved with me, as if calling for me, wanting to be petted.

I smiled, imagining these flowers back at the shop. If we sold well before, with these flowers, we would be the hot new thing.

My smile faded.

The shop was probably gathering dust now. My mother was gone, and I would never go back to the human world. There was nothing waiting for me there anymore—that realization hit me hard.

"What is it?" Ash asked, appearing by my side.

I shrugged. "So much happened in the past few weeks."

Ash nodded. "So much changed in the past few weeks."

"Yup," I muttered. "I don't think I could go back home now, even if I wanted to."

Ash's brows slanted down. "Do you still think about that?"

"Sometimes," I confessed. "But with my mother gone, I would only have the shop there." I opened my arm, gesturing to the entire meadow. "But I have all the flowers I could possibly want here, so even the shop doesn't feel right anymore."

"What does feel right?"

"I don't know," I whispered. When he had kissed me, that had felt right. The two of us together. But when he pulled back and kept on ignoring me, I started believing I was wrong about that. "But it isn't as if I have a choice, right? Being queen is the next step, doesn't matter what I want."

"Hayley...." Ash let out a long breath. "I never wanted you to feel like you have no other choice. If you want to go back, all you have to do is tell me. It'll hurt, I'll try to convince you otherwise, but I'll take you back."

I frowned. "It'll hurt? Why? Because the Spring Court

won't have a queen to take over the throne when you defeat Vasant?"

He stared at me, those deep green eyes going straight for my soul. Holy shit, this wasn't fair. "It would hurt more than you could ever imagine," he said, his voice rough, almost husky.

A shiver rolled down my spine. I shook my head. "Don't do this."

"Do what?"

I took a step back, needing some space from him. "Don't look at me like you want me, and don't say things you don't mean." He lowered his gaze, and I felt a knife cutting through my heart. There he went, the perfect warrior who obeyed his queen. I had told him to not look at me like that, and he instantly averted his eyes. "Please, let's go back."

"I brought you here to relax," he objected.

Relax? He wanted me to relax? I hadn't really relaxed since I met him. The frustration, the fear, the apprehension, the shame I had been feeling in the past weeks filled my chest, rising to my throat, and escaping my mouth as words I wasn't ready to say. "I can't relax, Ashton. Not for one minute, for one second. When you aren't with me, I worry about you the entire freaking time. Is he safe? Was he found out? Did anyone else betray him? And when you're with me...." I clenched my hands at my sides. "When you're with me, I can't breathe. I feel it in here." I bumped my fist twice on my chest. "Something pulling me toward you. Even though you ignore me, I keep waiting for any sign, any spare look, or a nonexistent smile." I shook my head. "Why are you avoiding me? Are you disappointed that I am Eden's daughter? Did you wish for someone else? Someone better?"

Ash frowned. "What?"

"Do you hate me that much? You can't stand me? Is that it?"

Ash snorted. "Are you serious?"

I glared at him. "Why do you think I'm joking?"

"For leaves' sake...." He ran his hand over his hair, mussing it up. "I'm avoiding you because it's too blooming painful to be near you and not be able to touch you, to kiss you."

I blinked. "What? I thought you...."

"I'm crazy about you, Hayley. When I'm with you, I live in a constant battle for control, because if it were up to me...." He clamped his mouth and shook his head.

"Tell me," I urged, dying for his words like a thirsty person in a desert. "This is your queen's orders. Tell me."

Ash fixed those green eyes on mine. "If it were up to me, I would stay by your side and hold your hand every single second of the day. If it were up to me, I would make sure you're always smiling. If it were up to me, I would have told you how I really feel and made love with you since before the first time we kissed."

My heart stopped, and my breathing caught. "Then why don't you?" I asked, my voice a thin rasp.

"I can't." He shook his head again. "I shouldn't...."

This freaking "can't" and "shouldn't" again. "General Ashton, look at me." It took him a moment, but Ash lifted his chin and his eyes found mine again. "Is this a matter of life and death? Will you or I die if you don't stay away from me?"

His brows turned down. "I don't think so, but—"

"That's good enough for me." I straightened and marched to him. I placed my hand over his heart, and he went still. "Ashton," I started, trying to be bold, the boldest I had ever been. I swallowed hard. A pained look crossed

Ashton's eyes, and his heartbeat accelerated under my palm.

I couldn't ignore how wonderful and warm his skin felt. I wanted to slide my hand under his tunic, run my fingertips up and down his chest, tracing each of his muscles, feeling them contract and expand with my touch.

My fingers twitched, and I licked my lips. His gaze followed my tongue, his green eyes darkening. He pressed his eyes shut and growled.

I gave in and slipped my hand under his tunic, letting my fingers trail his six-pack and that glorious V muscle leading down into his trousers. My other hand followed suit, and when my fingertips grazed the waist of his pants, Ashton inhaled sharply and wrapped his hands around my wrists, stilling my fingers.

"What are you doing?" he asked, his voice rough.

I blurted out before I lost my courage, "General Ashton, as your queen, I order you to make love with me."

His eyes went round. I could see the tension in his jaw and his shoulders as he worked this out in his head. Come on, there was nothing to think about. He just had to feel.

I was about to yell at him that he was a horrible general for not obeying his queen, when he groaned and tugged me closer, erasing the distance between us.

He brushed his lips over mine once, twice, three times, as if he needed to test the waters before actually jumping in deep. But then he jumped in, his mouth moving with a rough want against mine. I matched his rhythm, showing him I was ready. His tongue invaded my mouth, dancing with mine, and I moaned. With a groan, he knotted his hand in the hair at my neck, pressing me to him even more.

I heard the rustle of leaves beside us, and startled, I broke the kiss and searched for the source of the noise. But it was just Ash, working his magic and creating a bed of sorts on the ground, made of smooth leaves.

I faced him, and Ashton seemed to hesitate. "My queen, are you sure?"

Holy shit. I answered him, but not with words.

I tugged on his shirt and pulled it over his head, throwing it aside somewhere on the forest floor. Then I slipped my own dress down my body.

Ash watched me with those beautiful green eyes. His gaze raked every inch of my body, as if he wanted to etch my image into his mind so he could never erase it, even if he wanted to.

I felt it then, the pull that usually called me to him, the tug in my chest that told me this wasn't just a hot attraction. There was more going on between us, and this was the first step to finding out what it was. Holy shit, I really wanted to find out.

Slowly, Ash snaked his hands around my waist and leaned over me, kissing me again.

His kiss started slow and deep, but when I entangled one of my legs around his, he groaned and his kiss became rougher, as if he couldn't get enough of me.

He slid his hands down to my thighs and tugged them. I wrapped my legs around his waist, and he lowered us to the makeshift bed.

He kept an elbow on the bed so his weight wasn't crushing me, but that was exactly what I wanted. I pushed his ass with the heel of my foot, pressing him closer. Groaning, he dropped the elbow and buried his face in my neck. He inhaled before placing a sweet kiss on the soft spot between my neck and shoulder. I shivered again. Chuckling, he bit that same spot, making me shiver yet again.

I was about to protest that he still had his pants on, when his hand trailed a path to my inner thigh. I stopped breathing, suddenly aware of how bad this could go, how involved I could become, how taken I would be, but I was not capable of stopping right now.

He propped himself on his elbow and looked at me. His fingers neared my entrance, and I arched my back, closing my eyes. He thrust not one but two fingers inside me, filling me with sudden immense pleasure. I gasped, taken aback by the friction.

"Holy shit," I whispered.

He rubbed his thumb on my clit, and I cried out, digging my nails in his shoulders. He drew circles around me while sinking his fingers deeper, sending fire rolling in waves in my veins. Moans escaped my throat, but that was something I couldn't control, especially when Ash was watching me with his mouth slightly parted, his breathing heavy, and his eyes shining as if I were the most beautiful, the most delicious thing he had ever seen.

My toes curled, and I arched my back, feeling the pleasure building, so close to exploding.

Then he stopped everything.

"What...?" I asked, but he raised a brow at me before moving down, placing tiny kisses on my neck, shoulder, breast, belly, and hip. My breath caught.

Ash spread my legs apart and leaned into me, teasing me with his hot breath along my inner thighs, making my belly clench in anticipation. Then his tongue lashed out on my clit, and I cried his name. I fisted the vines around me, afraid I would break into a million pieces with each stroke of his tongue. Then he slid two fingers inside me hard while circling his tongue around my clit, and I was done for. My body tightened, and pleasure broke loose like a dam, making my body quiver uncontrollably.

For a moment, I was in a blissful daze, and when I started to come down from my high, I found Ashton taking off his trousers. I looked at his cock and swallowed hard. He was huge, and I couldn't wait another second before he was inside me.

"Do you need me to order you to come over here?"

He let out a soft chuckle as he crawled over me. Keeping most of his weight on his elbows, he rested his forehead on mine, and as I spread my legs, he positioned himself at my entrance. I grabbed his biceps as he entered me, robbing me of air and filling me completely. When he was deep inside me, buried to the hilt, he stilled.

"This feels so good," he muttered. "You feel so good."

I wrapped my legs around his waist and kicked his fine ass. "Ash, I'm going to die if you don't move."

His lopsided grin flashed on his lips before he brought them to mine. Kissing me, he pulled all the way out—making me feel his absence—and then sank back inside me. He did it again and again, going faster and deeper with each stroke, making me scream louder and louder.

This was too good, holy shit, just too good. Sex had never been this good. I didn't know what it was, but I felt so close to him, so connected to him. He kissed my neck, his warm breath on my skin and his delicious scent filing my lungs, sending a shiver up my spine.

He bit my neck. "I could eat you up," he said with a growl.

Oh, please do.

With each thrust, my body tightened with pure pleasure, and I was sure that, if he kept that rhythm, I wouldn't last much longer, and damn, I wanted this to last. Surprising him,

I pushed him to the side and flipped us around. His eyes widened as I sat straight over him.

I smiled, and then he smiled. A full-on smile. Just for me. My heart stuttered.

His hands landed on my waist, and with my eyes locked on his, I started moving. I pulled up, then down hard. He groaned, and his fingers curled in my skin.

"For the petal's sake," he mumbled as I moved up and down, harder and faster.

Even swimming in pleasure, I couldn't *not* appreciate the view under me. He was too hot, too handsome. His abs, chest, and biceps were big and taut. His chin and jaw chiseled, his cheekbones high, his parted mouth swollen and kissable, his hair soft and messy, messier than usual. His green eyes bright, staring at me. I had no idea what was written in them. I just knew that I couldn't stop. I couldn't stop staring at him, and I couldn't stop moving. Faster and harder.

"Hayley, please, don't stop," he said, his hands on my hips, guiding me.

I leaned down, wanting to be close to him, as close as we could be, when we both came. I placed a soft kiss on his lips, but then his hand was on my neck, locking me there. I wiggled my hips while moving them up and down, feeling my pleasure at the edge, and he groaned.

"Like that?" I asked, wiggling again.

"Oh, yes," he whispered.

He nudged my neck lower and took my mouth with his, plunging his tongue in and caressing mine. I wiggled one more time and lost it. I exploded but didn't stop moving. Although, with two more strokes, Ash went still for a second before trembling under me. He wrapped both arms around me as he rode down the high, and I smiled, glad I had done this to him, that I had made him come undone.

I rested my elbows on his chest and looked at him. "Was it so bad to give in to me?"

"You know, it wasn't bad at all," he said, running his hands down my back. "Quite the opposite, actually."

"Then why do you avoid me so much?"

He stared at me for a moment, his eyes growing serious. "I won't avoid you anymore, Hayley." He gulped hard. "I can't ignore you anymore."

MY HEART and my mind were torn in two. I wanted to surrender to Hayley completely, but Mahaere had warned me to stay away from her, to not tell her anything, and even though I hadn't said anything about the bond, I had just confessed how I truly felt. I had shown her.

Truth was, I wasn't strong enough to resist Hayley anymore. When we came back to the inn last night, I made my way to the floor, trying to act like an honorable fae, but Hayley held my hand in hers and pulled me to bed with her.

I thought I had been satisfied when we had made love in the forest but, in the flower's name, was I wrong. The moment she tugged on my tunic, the heat and desire spread over my body anew. I quickly got rid of my clothes, and hers too, lay down over her in the bed, and slipped my cock inside her, filling her.

I groaned as I started moving, the friction painful and delicious at the same time. Hayley scratched her nails over my back, and I bit down on her shoulder, wanting more, needing more, doing more.

Having sex for the first time, or second, with my mate after fifteen years of celibacy was just too much. Too good. Too perfect. I screwed her hard, until her nails were buried in my skin and her screams died out because she was lost to the bliss of her pleasure. When I came, she came with me.

I held her while our bodies trembled away the climax.

"Good night, Ash," she whispered, her mouth on my shoulder as she let the sleep take her.

I hadn't slept in a soft mattress in almost fifteen years, but who said I could sleep when the woman who had stolen my heart, who had my entire soul, pressed her naked body against mine and buried her face in my neck. She slept for a few hours while I watched over her, completely enamored, with my heart full for the first time in... forever.

I still didn't feel worthy of her, but the idea of sending her away and seeing her with someone else was like a knife to the gut. Soon, Hayley would be queen, and what would I be? She didn't even know I was her mate.

I shook my head slightly, making Hayley stir in my arms. I smoothed my hand down her back, and she settled down again, her breathing growing deeper. It was stupid of me to think about the future. I would be the servant who cleaned the floor that she walked upon, as long as I could stay close to her.

For leaves' sake, I just knew the goddesses would try to kill me next time one of them came over—in a few hours, when we had to get ready for the ball.

Meanwhile, I enjoyed Hayley's company.

I let her sleep in, and when she woke up, I brought her breakfast in bed.

Wrapped in the bedsheet, she sat up and smiled at the

tray I deposited over the mattress beside her. "What's going on?"

I shrugged. "Just wanted to do something nice for you."

She smiled at me, her sea-green eyes shining. "You do a lot of nice things for me."

I frowned. Did I? Until a few hours ago, I had acted like a jerk one too many times, but that was just because I was trying to honor my promise to the goddesses. Thinking about that made me feel shameful. What warrior broke his promises? I sure hoped the goddesses understood.

After eating, Hayley and I got dressed and we worked on last evening's promise: we set up the stand in the center of the village with plenty of food and medicine for the struggling fae. By the time we arrived, there were already over thirty fae waiting. We helped them in no time, but kept telling them we would close at noon because we had somewhere to be.

As the minutes passed and the word spread of our limited time, more and more fae showed up. From what we heard, fae from another village further south had heard what Hayley had been doing and came to get help too.

That worried me a little. If the next village had heard about Hayley and her kindness, how long would it take for soldiers to hear it and for the word to reach the fake king's ears? Even if he didn't know Eden's daughter was the one behind this, he certainly wouldn't leave it alone. He would send the soldier to arrest us, if not kill us in front of the fae so they knew better than to rebel.

I just didn't take her away from here right this instant because soon this would be done. Besides only helping in the morning, tonight we would start the war. If Hayley were to help others, it wouldn't be here or this way. Tonight, everything would change.

The hours flew while Hayley and I helped the fae. It warmed my core to see her like this, feeding her people and taking care of them without prejudice. If she followed her heart, she would be an amazing queen.

When the warm sun was right above our heads, Mahaere showed up. She approached us using a glamour and helped us pack. The fae protested and asked Hayley to stay.

"We'll continue helping you," I said honestly. "We'll be back, don't worry."

After we were done, Hayley and I turned to the inn, but Mahaere shook her head at us. "Come with me," she said with a big smile.

Why did I get the feeling I would regret this?

We followed her past the inn and out of the village. We entered the forest and walked for about five minutes, until a small clearing appeared. In the center of the clearing was a big tent of green and golden fabric.

Four floral nymphs ran out the tent, smiling just as much as Mahaere.

"What's going on?" I asked, wary.

"We'll get you ready for the ball tonight," Mahaere said, sounding excited. "Come on." She grabbed Hayley's arm and pulled her inside the tent.

For leaves' sake....

I followed them in.

I gawked at the tent. This wasn't a tent. This was a mini castle with a wide room full of rugs, low velvet couches, and pillows. More fabric divided the tent into several rooms.

"I would ask the nymphs to help you wash up, but I know you'll refuse, so go." Mahaere pointed to one of those rooms. "Clean up, get dressed, and come back here soon. We have no time to waste."

Frowning, I watched as Mahaere and the nymphs took Hayley to the other side of the tent. She shot me a soft smile, as if she was sorry for me, but I knew she wasn't. Being pampered like this was probably a nice change for any woman—fae, human, vampire, whatever.

With a sigh, I went into the other room and began getting ready.

KNOWING Mahaere would take her sweet time with Hayley, I took a long bath, then shaved and touched up my hair, which was starting to get too long again, and dressed up in a yellow tunic and jacket and gold pants, with a thick golden sash around my waist—the Summer colors.

I didn't have to wait alone for too long in the first room. Though, instead of Hayley, Mahaere showed up first.

She smiled at me. "Dashing."

I straightened, knowing very well why she came to me. "Mahaere—"

She raised a hand, though her smile didn't fade. "Spare me the details. I understand the pull you feel for her is too much to endure. The most important thing now is to not tell her that you're her mate. Not yet."

My shoulders deflated. "Is it just because you think it'll freak her out, or is it because of something else?"

"It's for her," Mahaere said simply. "Do you understand?"

I wanted to argue with her, but holy petals, she was a goddess. I nodded. "I understand."

"Good." She turned her back to me.

Two seconds later, Hayley stepped out of the other room with the nymphs.

My jaw dropped, and my breath caught.

Hayley looked like a goddess herself, a Summer goddess bathed in light. She wore a yellow gown with a tight bodice, low cleavage, and a long, flowy skirt. Pieces of thin fabric in several shades of yellow wrapped around her waist and arms, and two long pieces fell down her back, like a cloak.

Her hair had been braided all over and bunched up at the nape of her neck. Long, golden earrings adorned her ears. Her face had been painted, but just enough to accentuate her natural beauty.

"You're... beautiful," I whispered, completely enamored. An invisible hand squeezed my heart, and words I couldn't say clogged my throat.

With a smile, Hayley twirled around. "Well, I gotta say, yellow was never my color, but Mahaere and the nymphs did a great job." Then she stopped and ran her eyes over me. Unlike her, I was sure I looked ridiculous in such a bright color. "It seems you clean up well too."

Such simple words, such a mild compliment, and yet I felt proud. Had I cleaned up well enough to stand beside a queen? For leaves' sake, I hoped so.

"Now I just need to glamour you two," Mahaere said. She stepped in front of Hayley and worked her magic. Hayley's skin darkened until it seemed she spent too much time under the baking Summer Court sun, and her hair turned dark brown. Her eyes also went from sea-green to Hayley.

Next, Mahaere glamoured me with the same traits.

"Being a Summer Court warrior suits you," Hayley said, throwing another compliment at me. I could get used to this.

"Your sword," Mahaere said, pointing behind me.

"Right." I picked up my sword from the table I had set it down on before and showed it to her. The goddess ran her hand over it, transforming the green-hued metal into pure gold. I blinked, not used to such brightness. But more than changing colors, Mahaere changed its size too.

"Weapons aren't allowed in the ballroom," the goddess said. "Hide this under your clothes. Only reach for it again when it's time, since it'll return to its normal configuration."

"Thanks," I said, tucking the sword-turned-dagger in the waist of my pants.

Mahaere glanced at Hayley and me. "Are you two ready?"

Hayley's eyes met mine for a minute—just a brief moment, but it said so much. *Are you ready? Can we do this? We are in this together, right?*

Always.

I nodded at Mahaere. "We're ready."

ABOUT HALF AN HOUR EARLIER, Mahaere and the nymphs had left, and the reality of what we were about to do came crashing down on me. I was a nervous wreck while Ash and I waited for the carriage to come pick us up. I paced inside the tent, twisting my hands around my dress.

After a few minutes, Ash halted in my path, towering over me. "Breathe in, breathe out," he instructed, doing it himself. I followed his lead. He reached over and ran his warm hands over my arms. "It'll be okay. I won't let anything happen to you."

How could he be so sure of that? We were walking into the lion's den willingly. A lot of things could go wrong.

I stepped into him. "Just hold me."

He didn't hesitate. In a flash, his arms were around me, and he pulled me into a tight embrace. "Everything will be okay," he whispered to me, but for some reason I believed he was saying that to himself too.

As promised, the carriage came to us. A dark-skinned coachman dressed in a pale yellow uniform appeared at the tent's opening, asking us to come with him. The carriage, also yellow with golden accents, stood just beside the tent. The coachman helped us inside, where two other fae waited for us.

"Hayley, let me introduce you to Queen Natsia and Prince Varian of the Summer Court," Ash said as we sat down across from them inside the carriage.

The queen smiled at me. "Nice to meet you, Queen Hayley. May I say the Summer Court colors suit you very well?"

"Um, thank you," I mumbled, suddenly stunned. I had never met royalty before, and these two seemed like the epitome of nobility, beauty, richness, and charm.

The queen was an elegant female fae with dark skin, lustrous brown hair twisted in an intricate bun behind her head, and warm hazel eyes. She wore a beautiful golden gown and a heavy golden crown atop her head. The prince wasn't much different. In a way, he reminded me of Ash with his wide shoulders and tall frame. His skin was a little lighter than his mother's, and his eyes were a fascinating dark green, darker than Ash's. His hair was long and dark, tied in a loose ponytail behind his back. He wore a pale yellow tunic, golden pants, and a beige jacket, all perfectly tailored.

"Are you ready for your first ball in the fae realm, Queen Hayley?" Prince Varian asked with a small smile.

I frowned, not liking the way they were addressing me. I wanted to open my mouth and ask them to stop, but I didn't, because if I were to succeed tonight, if we were going to win, then I would become queen, even if only for a while. I had to get used to it.

"Not really," I said, twisting my hands in my dress again.

Queen Natsia chuckled. "She's honest. I like it."

The carriage lurched forward as we started moving.

The queen, the prince, and Ash made small talk while we rode to the Spring Court's capital. They talked about the weather, the people, the upcoming celebrations, and then the subject changed to the current situation.

Queen Natsia related that her spies told her Vasant's army was still growing at a rapid pace and trained nonstop. They truly believed Vasant was up to something, but since none of them were high ranked in the Spring Court, they couldn't find out what exactly he was doing.

"Hopefully, he won't have time to execute his plans," Prince Varian said.

The conversation went on as Ash told them about the situation in the Spring Court—he told them about the abandoned villages, the starving and sick fae, and that Vasant had been hunting me and killing young female fae who looked like me.

My stomach revolved with the memories of the witch, Sanna, killing the young girls in that village. Never again. Hopefully, after tonight, that wouldn't happen ever again.

I lost track of the conversation when I looked outside the carriage window and saw Greentref, a sprawling town with beige houses covered in green ivy and brown roofs, cobblestone streets, and lesser fae going about their business as if the other villages in the Spring Court weren't suffering.

But what really snatched my attention was the building atop a green hill. The Evergreen Palace was a massive castle made of brown stone and wood, with tall towers and vines covering almost every inch of its sides.

Soon, we crossed through the main street of Greentref and entered the palace's ground. The carriage came to a stop right in front of the castle's main entrance.

"Welcome home," Ash whispered in my ear before helping me out of the carriage.

I stared at the palace before me, my heart going a million miles a second. This was supposed to be home. It sounded like a fairy tale gone wrong, didn't it?

I didn't have much time to think about it as we were escorted inside. I gawked at the ample foyer with its dark green stone flooring, wood paneling, and the huge golden chandelier hanging from the impossibly tall ceiling. At the wide hallways, which matched the foyer in decoration, with beautiful landscape paintings on the walls. At the tall golden double doors that led to the ballroom. At the ballroom with its many round tables, green tablecloths, pink or blue or yellow flowers as a centerpiece, the stone stairs at the other side of the large room that opened up in some sort of landing, where a band played slow music to the side.

At the fae standing around the tables, of every color and shape, all of them different and beautiful in their own way.

As Ash guided me to our table, I easily recognized the king of the Winter Court and his queen and mate. King Cadewyn had long white hair, loose around the fur cloak over his shoulders. His eyes sparked blue like the deep ocean. As a true king of Winter, he wore a white shirt, jacket, and pants. Beside him, Queen Amber was a contrast, but equally enchanting. Once a human turned fae, Amber had long, black hair and fair skin. Her silver gown hugged her perfect form, and at the moment I envied her elegance and beauty.

"Queen Hayley," Queen Amber said, embracing me tight. "I understand how jarring it is coming from the human world and being dropped here." She pulled back and fixed her bright green eyes on mine. "If you need help with anything, or simply someone to talk to, know that I'm here."

I smiled at her. "That means a lot, thank you."

Ash bowed his head to King Cadewyn, but the king scoffed at him and patted Ash's back hard. Prince Varian stood beside them, and I couldn't take my eyes off them.

"Aren't they quite a sight?" Queen Amber said in a low voice.

I glanced at her. "They truly are." Calvin Klein would have given up half his fortune to have these three posing for his underwear collection, for sure.

Though the three of them were impossibly tall and wide and plain hot, my heart kept pulling toward only one. Ashton. Even though he wasn't of royal blood like the other two men, he could have fooled me. Ash was made of pure honor and strength. Otherwise, how could one endure a decade and a half of torture and still be loyal to one's king?

"I know that look," Amber said with a smile.

I smoothed out my expression. "What look?"

"That I'm-falling-in-love look." She winked at me.

"Um, what?" I glanced around, not sure what say or do. It wasn't as if I hadn't thought about it, I just didn't want to admit it. It was too damn soon, and there was still an arduous path ahead of us.

A waitress stopped by our circle and offered glasses with champagne. I took a flute from her and downed a big gulp.

Ash stepped to my side. "Be careful with that. You're half-fae, but we still have to figure out just how fae alcohol affects you. Besides, we all need to be clearheaded for what is ahead."

"I know, but I don't think one glass will put me over the edge," I said, taking another sip.

Two other male fae stepped in our circle. I was introduced to them—General Kei from the Winter Court, and

General Behar from the Summer Court. Next, I was introduced to a couple standing by the table beside ours: Altan and Zora, the king and queen of the Dawn Court, which stood right between the Spring and the Summer Courts.

According to Ash, Altan and Zora had joined our cause and were here to support us. All of this scared me a little, because Ash had told me these royals never came to any of Vasant's gatherings, and now they were all here, along with their best generals and a bunch of their royal guards. Wouldn't that make Vasant suspicious?

Hopefully, the fake king was so wrapped up in himself, he didn't notice anything.

"It seems we might finally get the numbers we need," I said in a low voice.

"I think so," Ash answered.

Suddenly, the musicians stopped playing. A set of double doors by their side opened, and a tall man with short, blond hair stepped through. He was dressed in pompous, bright green and golden attire, with a golden crown atop his head—my father's crown.

My crown.

That witch, Sanna, was right by his side, not looking one bit different from the other day. Black hair messy all around her, a black gown, and a sneer on her red lips.

Another male fae followed them. "That's General Xuan," Ash told me. Though his voice was barely a whisper, I could hear the rage in his words. I remembered seeing him outside the diner, right before Ash and I came to the fae realm.

"Welcome, my friends," Vasant said with a smile, atop of the stairs landing. "It's an honor to celebrate fifteen years of my reign with all of you." He gestured to the musicians. "Please, keep the music going." He waved at the waitresses around the room. "Keep the drinks coming. Let's have some fun." Holding that smile, Vasant descended the stairs with his witch and his general close behind him.

The fake king started going around the room to greet everyone.

And I began hyperventilating.

Ash took a step closer to me, gluing his side to mine. "Deep breaths," he whispered.

I glanced at him. "How are you so calm?"

"Believe me, I'm not," he said, his voice tight. "But I'm better at not showing it."

I groaned and let out a long breath. I tried distracting myself by looking around the ballroom, from the amazing details on the window frames of many thin vines entwined together, to the darkening skies outside, to the perfectly set table and centerpieces, to the beautiful fae, the fancy gowns, the ridiculous hairstyles.

"Get ready," Ash whispered to me.

I stilled myself as I turned and saw Vasant greeting King Altan and Queen Zora. Then he moved on to King Cadewyn and Queen Amber, both of whom seemed uncomfortable with the situation. I reminded myself that Vasant had mistreated Queen Amber when visiting the Winter Court not long ago, and somehow King Cadewyn didn't kill him. It must be hard for both of them to be here, smiling at the fake king as if they were good friends.

Vasant spun to the Summer Court royals—us. From beside me, I could feel Ash's body trembling. It was probably hard for him too, more than I first considered, to be here, standing in front of the fae who killed his king and captured him.

I inhaled deeply. If Ash could do this, so could I.

Vasant bowed his head to Queen Natsia and Prince Varian. "It's so good to see you both," he said with a smile. "Like I told King Cadewyn, I hadn't expected you all to come to celebrate with me, but I'm thrilled you're here." He turned his smiling face to Ash and me. "And who might you two be?"

"These are my cousin's kids," Queen Natsia said. "Andre and Hanna," she lied, the words firm and confident, just like a queen should be.

Ash bowed his head to the fake king. "It's a pleasure to meet you, King Vasant."

I curtsied at him, but didn't dare say anything, sure my voice would break or I would say the wrong thing, thus giving away our disguise.

"My, oh, my, Lady Hanna, may I say, you're quite stunning." He reached for my hand and kissed the top, all the time holding my gaze. My stomach revolved with disgust.

"Thank you," I forced myself to say.

I let out a relieved sigh when he moved on to the next group.

"You did well," Ash said to me.

"You too." I frowned. "That was sure harder for you than for me."

He offered me a tight-lipped smile, the most I ever got from him. My heart skipped a beat.

Not long after, the music grew louder and Vasant took Sanna for a dance. When the second song started, other couples joined the fake king and his witch on the dance floor.

Prince Varian took his mother for a spin, and King Cadewyn danced with his mate.

With a half smile, Ash extended his hand to me. "May I have the pleasure of this dance?"

I smiled at him. "Always."

I slipped my hand into his and let him take me to the dance floor. He put both his hands on my waist, I brought my arms around his shoulders, and we began dancing, swaying side to side with the beat of the music.

"Despite the situation, I'm glad to be here, in the Evergreen Palace with you," Ash said, his dark eyes fixed on mine. "Soon, you'll be able to call this place home."

I didn't want to think about that, because honestly, the life of a queen scared the hell out of me. I wasn't elegant enough, knowledgeable enough, firm enough. I didn't have a steel back and a soft heart. In the flower shop, my mother and I never had other employees, except for some delivery guy once every blue moon, because I didn't feel like ordering others around. But now I was supposed to rule an entire kingdom?

I shuddered with the thought. "Can we change the subject?"

Ash frowned. "What shall we talk about?"

I shrugged. "Anything that takes my mind off the plan." The plan that should be set in motion in just another hour or two.

"Let's see," Ash said, with a rare teasing tone. Then he grew serious, his eyes searching mine. "Hayley, I need to tell you something."

Tell me something? My heart sped up. "What?"

"Um, I... in the flower's name, this isn't easy." He exhaled loudly. "Hayley, I—"

"Sorry to interrupt," someone to our side said. Ash and I halted in shock, and my eyes went wide upon seeing the fake king standing beside us. He offered his hand to me. "But would you mind if I had a turn?"

My insides stiffened. Ash's nostrils flared, and his jaw ticked.

I wanted to say a big, fat no to him, but I believed it would only make things worse. With a forced smile, I let go of Ash and slipped my hand into his. "It's my pleasure."

The fake king snaked his arm around my waist, pulling me close, while holding my right hand out. With a satisfied smile to Ash, he spun us away.

"I have to say, ever since laying eyes on you earlier, I've been entranced," he said with a honeyed smile. My stomach tightened, and I thought I would throw up at his feet. Holy shit, this was not only my father's murderer but also my uncle. "I had to dance with you."

"Um, thank you" was all I could say to him.

Dancing with him was as uncomfortable as prying out my fingernails with a sewing needle, but I believed I put on a good show. I let him guide me around the ballroom without resistance and smiled at him every few seconds, like a perfect little submissive court lady.

In about an hour or two, he was in for a big surprise.

He led us back to the center of the dance floor.

And he surprised me.

Vasant spun me under his arm and pulled me back to him, my back to his chest.

He pressed a dagger against my throat. "Did you think you could fool me, Hayley?"

ASHTON

ONE OF THE most difficult things I had to do in my entire life was to allow the fake king to take Hayley dancing. I wished I could have broken the glamour right then, stabbed my sword in his heart, and ended his ridiculous reign. But we had to wait until it was all ready. Until we could act.

So I swallowed my pride and my rage and stepped back, my heart tearing in two at seeing my mate dancing with my worst enemy.

I retreated to the edge of the dance floor and grabbed a flute of champagne from a waitress. I didn't plan on drinking it, but I didn't want to just stand there looking like I was up to something. So I pretended to sip from the flute while following Vasant's every move and watching where he took my mate. Across the dance floor, Sanna and General Xuan stood, also watching their king like two bodyguards.

Perhaps it was because our souls were connected, but I could easily see how nervous Hayley was at being so close to Vasant. If I could rescue her, I would. Holy petals, I would give them five more minutes; then I would stop them and ask to switch again. I didn't care if that wasn't polite or customary.

My skin prickled a second before the entire world turned upside down.

In the center of the ballroom, Vasant spun Hayley around and held her back against his chest.

With a dagger at her throat.

"Did you think you could fool me, Hayley?" he said, loud enough for half the fae in the ballroom to hear.

The music stopped, the fae quit dancing and retreated several steps, and my heart dropped.

I ran to Hayley.

Vasant shook his head at me. "If you want your mate to stay alive, I suggest you stay back, General Ashton."

I halted, my feet glued to the stone floor. I stared at Hayley, at her eyes wide at Vasant's revelation. This wasn't how I wished she found out about it, but there it was, the truth out in the open.

As if Mahaere's magic had an expiration date, our glamours faded away, and the guests gasped at us.

"What's going on?"

"Who is she?"

"Isn't that General Ashton? I thought he was dead!"

"What is King Vasant doing?"

"The fake king has really lost it."

The whispers spread like wildfire, but it all ceased when Spring soldiers swarmed the ballroom, securing the exits and forming a wide circle around us, their weapons ready to strike.

I faced the fake king with my allies right behind me. King Cadewyn, Queen Amber, General Kei, Queen Natsia, Prince Varian, General Behar, King Altan, and Queen Zora. At a moment's notice, the soldiers who had pledged their alliance to Hayley and me and the other courts' soldiers would storm the ballroom, and the war would officially start.

I fished my weapon from my back, my sword turning into its beautiful self upon contact, and pointed it straight at Vasant's head. "Let my queen go!"

"I don't think so," Vasant said, sounding too calm for the situation. "I'll kill her right in front of your eyes, just like I killed my brother. You'll feel helpless and hopeless all over again." He faced the royals behind me. "Then I'll kill everyone else who dares to stand up to me."

I heard a growl from King Cadewyn, who was probably eager to turn into his wolf and rip out Vasant's throat. Though I wouldn't mind seeing Vasant dead, I would be the one to do it. I would be the one to kill him.

"This is nonsense, Vasant," Queen Natsia said, taking a step forward. "Let's act like the civilized and educated fae we are and talk. I'm sure we don't need to resort to violence."

"Talk?" Vasant snorted. "Why? Do you think I'll hand my court to this half human just like that?" He shook Hayley, causing her to gasp and my heart to stop again. "You'll have to kill me first."

For leaves' sake....

"My pleasure." I whirled my sword in my hand and advanced.

A commotion started to the side. Fae parted, letting the Sanna walk by, dragging someone behind her.

"Here she is," Sanna said, throwing the fae at Vasant's feet as if she were a sack of potatoes.

On her knees and whimpering, the fae lifted her head. "I'm sorry."

My stomach dropped. "Nevena," I whispered, taking a

step back. The old female had a black eye and a split lip. Her hair was disheveled, and her clothes stained with blood. They had captured her. They had tortured her. "No."

"Did you think you could sneak messages to my soldiers and steal them to your side?" Vasant asked, smiling as if this was amusing. "One of my trusted soldiers intercepted her messages. He brought her in, and I've got to admit, she only revealed a small piece of your plan under severe torture. Such a resilient fae. Shame she's on your side." He kicked her stomach, making her fall on the stone floor. I winced, and Hayley whimpered. "With you gathering soldiers and the sudden appearance from the Dawn, Summer, and Winter Courts, it was easy to deduce what was happening."

In the flower's name....

We had planned to sneak into the palace with as many allies as we could—the royals from other courts, their soldiers, and the soldiers who had pledged to work with me against the fake king—spread around, attack Vasant, force his hand so his soldiers would retreat, kill the fake king and his generals, and take over the castle. Without a king or any other leading figure, the rest of the army would fall apart.

And Hayley would be here to pick up the pieces.

It had been a grand idea, a dangerous idea, but one that avoided a drawn-out and bloody war that would certainly hurt the Spring Court fae and devastate our kingdom.

But now it was all over. Vasant knew all about it, and he was ready with his many soldiers surrounding us.

And he had Hayley. If he killed her, this was all over. Even if we fought against him and won, there wouldn't be an heir to take the throne.

I lowered my sword.

Beside me, King Altan shook his head. "This wasn't what I signed up for," he muttered.

"Tell me, King Altan, what did you sign up for?" Vasant asked. "You thought you would come into the Evergreen Palace, run a sword through my heart, and be done with it?" King Altan opened his mouth, but no words came. So Vasant continued. "Since you seem unsure of this alliance, I'll offer you a new deal, King Altan." He paused, his lips spreading in a wicked grin. "Stand back and I won't harm you, your queen, or any of your soldiers."

I stared at King Altan. He fiddled with his hands, clearly considering this.

"You can't be serious, Altan," King Cadewyn hissed.

As if we didn't exist, King Altan lowered his head to Vasant. With his head still bowed, he took Queen Zora's hand and retreated to the corner of the ballroom, where he pretended nothing was happening.

What the blossom?

"Would anyone else like to strike a deal with me?" the fake king asked. "I'll promise to be considerate and think of this as a fleeting moment of weakness."

I glanced side to side, afraid King Cadewyn or Queen Natsia would fall into his trap, but King Cadewyn only glared at him, and Queen Natsia shook her head like a disappointed mother.

Perhaps all wasn't lost yet.

I raised my sword to Vasant again. "I'll repeat it just one more time. Let her go!"

The fake king snorted. "It's safer to say I'll kill her in the next second than let her—"

His words died out when the flowers from all the centerpieces flew to his face. They grew in length and thickness, winding around Vasant's body and taking over inch by inch.

Free, Hayley stepped back. "Holy shit, you talk too much!" She twisted her hands, and the flowers tightened around Vasant, causing him to grunt in pain.

Despite the situation, I smiled at her, amazed by her power and her boldness.

Though it didn't last. Vasant was too powerful. A moment later, he broke through the vine-like chains and advanced on Hayley.

Oh, not this time. I jumped forward, taking her wrist and pulling her to my side.

Then a battle started.

King Cadewyn transformed into his huge white wolf and lunged at Vasant. Prince Varian didn't waste time and went to help King Cadewyn, his fire magic at his fingertips. Queen Natsia attacked Sanna, while Amber and the generals dealt with the soldiers around the ballroom.

I wanted to hold on to Hayley and ask her if she was okay, but before I could, General Xuan came at me, his blade aimed at my head. I pushed Hayley aside and parried his attack with my own blade.

"It won't be that easy," I said with a snarl.

"We'll see about that," Xuan spat. He swung his blade at me, and I leaned back, avoiding the hit.

I ducked under another swing, stepped to the side, and brought my sword high over his head. The general was a good fighter and parried my strike with his arm—covered with his reinforced leather armor.

In that moment, I lost track of Hayley. But when I spun back, getting away from one of Xuan's moves, I found her not far from me. She was beside Queen Natsia as the both of them fought against the witch.

My step faltered.

I had known she would have to fight at some point. I couldn't protect her all the blooming time, but it wasn't easy to see her in the middle of the fray, especially when her first real opponent was a powerful witch.

Taking advantage of my distraction, Xuan came for my head. I quickly leaned back and brought my sword up, barely stopping his blade from cutting through my neck.

Enraged, I swung my sword wide, hitting his arm and creating an opening. Then I landed a hard front kick into Xuan's chest. He went down, skidding on the floor for a few feet.

I lunged at him, straddling his legs. "This gives me no pleasure," I said before burying my sword into his chest.

Xuan's body trembled before going limp on the floor. I stepped back, suddenly nauseated by all this fighting, all the deaths, all the treachery. But it would only end once the fake king and all of his allies were dead.

"Now!" Vasant cried.

I glanced up.

The witch whirled her hands and threw black sparks at Hayley and Queen Natsia. Hayley was able to duck and miss it, but Queen Natsia wasn't fast enough. The spark hit her right shoulder. Instantly, her body convulsed and she fell to the floor.

Prince Varian's face went pale. "Mother!"

He ran to her.

But he never reached her.

The witch twisted her hands again. A round, purple

portal appeared in Prince Varian's path. He tried to stop, but it was too late.

He crossed the portal and disappeared.

With a wicked smile, the witch closed the portal. "Who's next?"

"Oh, you bitch," Amber snarled. She threw her hands at the witch, and ice shards rained down at her. Assisting his mate, King Cadewyn abandoned Vasant and pounced on the witch.

In a flash, King Cadewyn ripped out the witch's throat, and blood poured down her chest.

Without his general and his witch, Vasant was practically alone in the ballroom. King Cadewyn, Queen Amber, Hayley, and I turned to Vasant, while Kei and Behar controlled the soldiers around the ballroom.

"It's over, Vasant," I said, once again aiming my sword at his chest. "Surrender and I promise you I'll give you a painless death."

Vasant spat at our feet. "Never!" He punched the air in front of him. The broken flowers on the floor shot up, becoming long vines coming for us.

But Queen Amber brought her arms up, raising a thin sheen of ice, slicing the vines in half. Meanwhile, King Cadewyn lunged at Vasant. Hayley used her own magic and tied vines around Vasant's wrists and ankles, keeping him in place.

Considerate of my desire, King Cadewyn didn't kill Vasant. He just bit his thigh, giving a nasty wound that would certainly make it hard for him to fight back.

With my eyes on his, I advanced on Vasant. "There's so much I could tell you, so much I could curse you, but I think your biggest curse will be to know you failed. You'll die, and

Hayley will become the queen. She'll make the Spring Court as great as her father made it. And we'll all forget you even existed."

He opened his mouth to say something, but I didn't give him the chance.

I pierced his heart with my sword.

Vasant's eyes went wide. Then his head lolled forward.

Hayley let go of the vines tying him, and his body flopped to the floor.

The fake king was dead.

But the fight was still going on around the ballroom.

I took Hayley's hand and shouted, "Stop!" Slowly, the fighting faded away. "The fake king is dead." I pointed to his body at our feet. "If you don't want to die, you should surrender right now." I didn't think trusting soldiers who willingly served Vasant was a good idea, but I wouldn't become an executioner and kill them all. I would figure out what to do with them later. "Hayley, daughter of King Eden, is here." Murmurs traveled through the ballroom. "The Spring Court will go back to the prosperous time it was before under her ruling. All you have to do is stop fighting and pledge your alliance to her."

Silence filled the ballroom for a moment.

The soldiers hesitated, but one by one, they all kneeled before Hayley. Once more I reminded myself that they could just be on their knees to avoid being killed. I would have to find a way to filter through the soldiers and give some purpose to the ones who couldn't be trusted.

Beside me, Hayley stilled, her cheeks growing red.

Now, she would have to get used being a queen.

FROM THE BALCONY, I watched the party in the garden below.

It had been a month since we defeated Vasant and his soldiers surrendered. The situation in the villages across the Spring Court was slowly getting better, but there was still a lot of work to do. Despite my protests to keep working nonstop, Ash had convinced me that it was time to take a short break, even if only for two days, and hold a real coronation ceremony. He said the fae were anxious to see me as the queen, to have a real ruler back.

"They need a strong figure," Ash had said, and I had almost laughed in his face. Strong figure? That wasn't me. But that didn't mean I wouldn't try my hardest to give the people all they wanted, all they needed.

So we held the coronation ceremony. We had invited all the royals from all courts, all noble families from the Spring Court, and I had insisted in having some lesser fae here too, even if their names had to be picked from a drawing of sorts. I wanted the lesser fae to know I was real, that I was here, and that I cared about them. The ones who attended the ceremony would go back to their villages and spread the word that I was on their side. That alone should make them less miserable, and soon I would make them much less miserable. With Ash, I had come up with a big plan to revitalize all villages and provide for the people—maybe not with money in their hands, but to create professions and opportunities. Everyone would have a rightful place.

The ceremony was held at the garden below, the biggest and most beautiful garden of the Evergreen Palace, and now my guests danced, chatted, and drank, all of them happy that Vasant was gone.

All of them but the Summer Court, who had sent a representative since Queen Natsia was in bad shape. That spell the witch had thrown at us had been poison, and it was now slowly spreading over the queen's body. According to the representative, they were trying all they could think of to stop or slow the process, but if things continued deteriorating, the Summer Queen only had a couple more weeks to live. Meanwhile, they were combing through Wyth—and other realms too—to find Prince Varian. King Cadewyn had said he only took a quick glance at the portal before it disappeared, but he remembered it being one that led to another realm.

If they couldn't find Prince Varian soon, the Summer Court could end up without a ruler.

That was certain to create more chaos.

Speaking of which, I found the flower shop and my house back on Earth in pure chaos when I went back there last week. It had been time to clean up everything, sell the shop and the house, close my life there, and move on. I had also brought my mother's body here and given her a proper burial. Now her eternal resting place was within walking distance, and I could visit her anytime I wanted.

"There you are."

I glanced over my shoulder and saw Ash stepping onto the balcony and walking to me. My breath caught at the sight of him, as it always did. He was wearing thick, dark green leather armor, his sword at his side, and his confidence all over himself. Handsome, strong, and hot were words that didn't even begin to describe how he looked.

"I was trying to hide from the *awful* party," I joked. The truth was, the damn crown now lying on the wooden rail was too heavy and I had come in to take something for the headache it was giving me. "But you found me."

He halted by my side, a half smile on his lips. "I'll always find you."

Ash had come a long way since he first escaped the dungeons. His nightmares were almost gone, and he rarely had a lapse with sudden and loud noises anymore. Soon, all of his suffering would be a distant memory.

What I would never forget, though, was that he had found out he was my mate a few days after bringing me to Wyth, but he hadn't told me, and he wouldn't have if Vasant hadn't blurted it out. After, Ash said that he planned on telling me, but only when I had the crown in my hands.

In my inexperience with this role, I had offered the crown to him, but he didn't accept it.

"I don't want to be the king," he had said. "Any least, not yet. Let me just be your general, your ally, and your mate."

My mate.

My heart expanded in my chest every time he was close to me, and I felt the connection linking us. I had felt it before, of course, but back then I hadn't known what it meant.

Now I knew, and I couldn't be more proud or happier to have him as my mate.

And all I wanted was to make him proud of having me as his.

Staring at the crown on the rail, Ash caught my hand and cradled it in both of his. "Already tired?"

"Not really." I explained to him about the headache.

"Oh, so I can't pounce on you right now?"

I lifted an eyebrow at him. "Right now? In the middle of the party?"

He shrugged. "It's not like we would be gone for the entire evening. It's just—" His eyes ran the length of me, as if he could see my body under this fluffy, dark green gown. "—you just look so delicious in that dress."

My cheeks heated. "Well...." I disentangled my hand from his, just so I could turn to him and wind my arms around his neck. "My headache isn't that bad. And even if it were, I'd never say no to making love with you."

A growl started low in Ash's chest. He hooked his arms around my back and turned us around, guiding us inside our bedroom.

He pushed us back until I was pressed against the wall. "Let's send this headache away then."

He cupped my face and kissed me, as if he was searching for the essence that gave him energy and sustained his life. His tongue ravished my mouth, and my knees weakened. I clasped my hands around his shoulders before I fell. But I wanted to. Shit, with him, I could fall headfirst.

Ash trailed kisses down my neck and over my collarbone. He stopped long enough to open the buttons of my dress and push it down, and then he kept going, kissing around my breast and down my belly. He pushed my dress past my hips and to the floor before standing straight, shrugging the top part of his uniform off, and pressing his body against mine.

I gasped when his mouth met mine, and he thrust his hips, his erection rubbing against me, making my core hotter and hotter. His hands slid around my leg and teased the edge of my panties. I whimpered, and he smiled against my lips. He rubbed his finger on me through the panties, drawing a moan from me.

"Do you want it?" he asked, his voice throaty. I dug my nails into his skin and gasped when he pulled my panties aside. "Do you want it?" he asked again.

"Please."

He sank a finger inside me, and I moaned. He buried his head in my neck and groaned with his mouth on my skin. "You're so wet."

Slipping his finger out, he then thrust two in. I arched my back, trying to give him better access to me. I didn't know what was better, the combination of his hot breath on my skin, the hand digging into my hip to keep me steady, his naked chest flush against mine, his cock rubbing against my leg, or the way he was touching me, driving me to the edge.

"So good," I whispered.

He rubbed his thumb on my clit and I burst. I trembled and whimpered, but he didn't let it go. He increased the pressure and kept thrusting those fingers inside me. I wanted to crawl inside myself, inside him, because there was no way I could survive this much pleasure, this much heat. A new wave hit me, and I screamed his name as I came.

With deft hands, Ash worked on his pants. I slapped his hands away and unbuttoned his pants myself, my eyes on his. I pulled his pants down enough to free his massive erection and closed my hand around him. A shiver assaulted his body, and a low growl rumbled from his chest.

He bent forward to kiss me, but I leaned back, wanting to

look at him while I stroked him, while I gave him pleasure. I ran my palm over him a couple of times before snaking my hand down and pushing his pants all the way to his feet.

I sank to my knees, and his gaze went wide. I smiled before clasping his hips and licking his cock from head to shaft and back.

"For the leaf's sake," he muttered, knotting his fingers in my hair.

I took him into my mouth, sucking hard, and he cursed some more. I felt him tensing, his fingers curling into my scalp with each stroke of my mouth, with each swirl of my tongue. I changed the rhythm, taking him in deeper and slower.

He shuddered. "Hayley," he gasped. I felt him coiling, his body stiffening, and I knew he was close. He cupped my face and pushed back, then pulled me to my feet.

I licked my lips. "I would have finished it."

His gaze followed my tongue, and he swallowed. "I know, but we can do that another time. Right now, I want to come inside you."

I shivered at his words, at the raw desire in his eyes. His arm wound around my waist, and he pressed me against the wall again. Not breaking his stare, I wrapped my legs around his waist, and he entered me, none too gentle. I cried out, arching my back to take him deeper, wanting—needing—the mix of pleasure and blissful pain.

"In the petal's name," he muttered as a shudder ran through his body. He closed his mouth over mine and assaulted me with his tongue. "I can't get enough," he whispered against my lips. "I can't get enough of you."

His words thrilled me, heated my core, and ignited the mating bond linking us.

Just then, his thrusts became harder and deeper, and I forgot just about everything else. All that mattered was this. Us. Together at this moment. I moaned, totally gone.

The heat wave was back and threatening to take me over any second. Holy shit, I wanted it to take me over. I wanted Ash to take me over right now.

"Ash," I gasped. "Please, don't stop."

He growled and bit my neck. Somehow, his thrusts became rougher, and I thought I was going to break into a million pieces of pure bliss. Then I did. My ecstasy exploded, and my legs turned into goo. With one more thrust, Ash joined me on the other side. He held me tight while his body convulsed, his head buried in my neck.

His quivers faded, and he brought his face to me. He kissed me long and gentle, taking my breath away. He didn't break the kiss while he lowered us to our bed, and we lay on our sides.

He placed butterfly kisses over my neck and shoulder, then sat up and reached for the covers. He brought them over us and lay on his back, tucking me under his arm. I rested my head on his shoulder and my hand on his chest. His heart still raced. I tilted my face to him and found him watching me.

Heat spread through my cheeks. "What?"

He kissed my forehead and tightened his arms around me. "How's the headache?"

I had completely forgotten about it. "Gone."

"Good." He offered me a half smile. "I don't think we're going back to that party."

I chuckled. "Why? Are you already ready for a second round?"

"Give me about two minutes, and then you'll find out."

Typical. Since the first time we made love, Ash had demonstrated an incomparable stamina. But I wasn't complaining. Making love to him, with my mate, was one of the best things in my life.

I nestled my head in his neck. "I love you, my warrior."

"I love you, my queen." He ran his hand over my back. "My mate."

Our story had started with a bang and lots of problems. There were still a lot of problems ahead of us, but I knew that as long as we stayed together, as long as Ash stood beside me as a warrior, as a king, or as my mate, we would overcome everything. We could do anything.

Even live a fairy tale romance.

———

CONTINUE READING stories in the Wyth Courts world! The next one is *Summer Prince* and you can pre-order it now!

THANK YOU

THANK you for reading *Spring Warrior*!

Did you like this book? Please, consider leaving a review on amazon and/or Goodreads, as reviews are very important to authors!

PRE-ORDER BOOK 3 NOW: *Summer Prince*

DON'T FORGET to sign up for my Newsletter to find out about new releases, cover reveals, giveaways, and more!

IF YOU WANT to see exclusive teasers, help me decide on covers, read excerpts, talk about books, etc, join my reader group on Facebook: Juliana's Club!

ABOUT THE AUTHOR

While USA Today Bestselling Author Juliana Haygert dreams of being Wonder Woman, Buffy, or a blood elf shadow priest, she settles for the less exciting—but equally gratifying—life as a wife, a mother, and an author. She resides in North Carolina and spends her days writing about kick-ass heroines and the heroes who drive them crazy.

Subscribe to her mailing list to receive emails of announcement, events, and other fun stuff related to her writing and her books: www.bit.ly/JuHNL

For more information:
www.julianahaygert.com

facebook.com/julianahaygert

twitter.com/juliana_haygert

instagram.com/juliana.haygert

goodreads.com/juliana_haygert

pinterest.com/julianahaygert

bookbub.com/authors/juliana-haygert

ALSO BY JULIANA HAYGERT

To find links and more info, go to:

www.julianahaygert.com/books/

The Blood Pact (Book 9)

The Wyth Courts

Winter King (Book 1)

Spring Warrior (Book 2)

Summer Prince (Book 3)

The Fire Heart Chronicles

Heart Seeker (Book 1)

Flame Caster (Book 2)

Sorrow Bringer (Book 3)

Earth Shaker (Novella)

Soul Wanderer (Book 4)

Fate Summoner (Book 5)

War Maiden (Book 6)

The Everlast Series

Destiny Gift (Book 1)

Soul Oath (Book 2)

Cup of Life (Book 3)

Everlasting Circle (Book 4)

Willow Harbor Series

Hunter's Revenge (Book 3)

Siren's Song (Book 5)

Breaking Series

Breaking Free (Book 1)

Breaking Away (Book 2)

Breaking Through (Book 3)

Breaking Down (Book 4)

Standalones

Daughter of Darkness